Baby Please Come Home To Me

A PRISON LOVE NOVELLA

BLAKE KARRINGTON

Chapter ONE

Rico's eyes were glued to the television in the rec room of the prison. *A Christmas Carol* was playing, and all of the eyes in the room were tuned in to the holiday classic. The room was full of felons, murderers, robbers, arsonists, you name it. It didn't matter what they'd done to land themselves in prison. They could have been deemed the worst people in the world in the eyes of others, but on this day, what they all had in common was the fact that they wanted just a piece of holiday spirit to infiltrate the hard grey prison walls. For a few hours they all became lost in the timeless tale. Memories of Christmases past invaded some of their minds. Some of them came from fucked up homes. Not all of them had gotten the chance to enjoy the kind of Christmas that you see on TV sitcoms, but that didn't mean they couldn't watch the movie and dream a little. Rico didn't speak the entire time that the movie was playing.

Once it was over, he snapped back into his grim reality and headed over to the wall lined with payphones, so he could call his girl, Charmaine. As he reached the beige wall, Rico's eyes connected with one of his fellow inmates, Chris.

"Yo' you been ducking a nigga for two days 'bout some noodles, homie. Let me find out, you like to partake in gambling, but you go ghost when it's time to pay up."

Rico had won three packs of noodles and two bags of potato chips fair and square in a card game, but Chris was acting like he didn't want to fork over the goods.

"Nah kid, it ain't even like that. I'm headed to canteen now. You gon' get ya little shit," he replied in his northern accent.

Rico smirked as he picked up the phone. "Now my shit little, but it's taking you two days to get me my lil' shit. That's tough." Rico shook his head and put in the information for his prepaid call. One thing he wasn't a stranger to out on the streets or in prison was fronting ass niggas. Shit, he even had to front himself every now and again. Difference was he never did it for bullshit, it was always a big bag at the end of the rainbow.

Rico leaned against the wall and licked his lips as he eyed a thick ass correctional officer named Candice. She looked like she was about to bust out of her uniform pants, and she was the cause for many erections in the prison camp. Rico had been down for four years and with his toffee-colored skin, honey-colored eyes, and his 6'4 muscular frame, he was eye candy among the CO's as well. He was handsome for sure. The brawny, tatted up thug, made panties moist most days just from the way he licked his lips and his slightly bow-legged stance. With hooded lids, he enjoyed the view while he waited on the call to connect. Finally, he heard the high-pitched voice that had become familiar to him over the last year.

"Hey baby, how's things going?" Charmaine spoke into the phone. Rico picked up right away on the fact that she sounded stressed, which wasn't new. Charmaine had two kids ages three and five by two different men, and both of them were dead-beats. She worked two jobs along with being a single mother and most days, she sounded like she needed a hug, a forehead kiss, some good dick, and a million dollars.

"Tell daddy what's wrong," Rico spoke in a low baritone tenor.

Charmaine sighed heavily. "Nothing. They just hit us with mandatory overtime today, and I'm just getting off. I swear it feels like I live at work, but I guess I should be grateful. I'm almost done with the kids' Christmas. At least if I can't give them time, I can give them toys," she mumbled.

Rico released a sigh of his own. "I swear I hate to hear you sounding like this. If I was there, you working two jobs would be out of the question. You damn sure wouldn't be outworking me and whenever I did get off, I'd come straight home to you to fuck the taste out your mouth, rub your feet, then rub your ass until you fell asleep. And I mean every night. I just need you to hang on ma. Your man is almost home."

Men in prison were optimistic at best because their idea of soon often meant more than a year. Rico had sixteen months left in his bid and for Charmaine that wasn't soon enough, but she was trying her best to hang in there.

"I know baby, and I can't wait." She was still holding onto three months ago when he got someone to give her $100. For as broke as she was at the time, that $100 may as well have been $1,000. She filled up her gas tank and got a much needed blowout. She didn't even have the money to get weave, but getting her natural shoulder-length hair done was just as good.

Hell her own trifling baby daddies couldn't even give her $100, so a man in prison doing it meant everything to her. It made Charmaine really feel like once he was back out in the real world, there was no limit to what he'd do for her and for that reason, she knew she just had to hold on until he came home.

"By the time I come home, just give me six months to stack my bread, and I want my seed. You know that, right?" Rico was thirty-two with no kids, and he wanted at least two of his own. Two kids were dragging Charmaine to hell and back, and she couldn't even imagine having four. But she wasn't telling Rico no. If she laid down and had two kids for two sorry ass niggas, then she could for sure have two for a man that would do right by her.

"I know. And as long as we're not struggling, you can have that."

Rico shook his head. "Come on ma. I'm not a lame out here. Struggling is something you'll never have to do with me. Never. Even on my worst days, me and my family gon' eat. I just need you to hold tight for a nigga. That's it. In fact, in the next few days, I'm gon' get my people to give you some more bread."

That was music to Charmaine's ears. She had been working more than she'd been doing anything else, so her next few paychecks were going to be lovely, but it felt good to be given money from a man. Her man. Charmaine knew that people thought she was dumb for holding down a man that she didn't even know before his bid. A year ago, she was visiting her cousin, Tookie, and Rico caught her eye. He was visiting with an older woman, and she assumed it was his mother. Rico was fine as hell, and he glanced over and caught her looking a few times. She was fine herself. And when she stood up, he observed her shapely 5'4 inch frame, flawless brown skin, her long ponytail was hanging down to her fat ass, and her thighs were thick as hell. Rico observed that she had a little pudge, but that didn't mean shit to a nigga like him. She had a body like a real woman. A grown woman.

Some women could be disrespectful as hell but with the way she kept looking over at him, Rico doubted that Tookie was her man. He wasn't a punk, but he didn't want unnecessary problems on the yard, so Rico wasn't even sure he should say anything. When he heard Tookie say that shorty was his cousin, he asked Tookie if she was single, and it went from there. Rico had a few females writing to him, but it was nothing major. After being down for almost four years, everyone except his mom had pretty much jumped ship. From their first conversation, Rico knew what time it was. Charmaine was struggling, so she wasn't that desperate female that would send him money. However he could tell she lacked self-esteem, and was desperately in need of some love. Some kind words from the sexy thug had her all in and after a month, she came to see him and had been his girl ever since. He knew that she caught flack for their relationship. People thought she was dumb, but their opinions didn't hold as much weight as the things he said to her.

Rico and Charmaine wrapped up their phone call, and he headed back to his pod as they called it. One thing prison had taught him was patience. He knew he just had to hold on a little while longer and if things went according to plan, he'd be set.

Chapter TWO

N icole gave her daughter the side eye as Charmaine cleaned up a mess that her son, Micha had made. "I still don't understand why you're not living in a house that someone left you." Nicole took a long drag from her cigarette. "If somebody left me a house free and clear, that's where I'd be."

Charmaine was glad that her back was turned towards her mother, so the woman wouldn't see her rolling her eyes. Charmaine thought every day about whether she should have stayed in the house, but she just didn't have the money to fix it up. The house was in terrible condition, there were issues that needed to be fixed that Charmaine couldn't fix like mold and a leaking roof. Also all the appliances needed to be replaced and the paint had totally peeled off the walls. Her father's mother had gotten sick a year ago and had to be put in a nursing home.

No one was able to keep the home up for her and when she died, she left it to Nicole. The house was in a neighborhood that was under heavy construction due to gentrification. A new group was moving in, and it seemed as if the old residences were being pushed out. When someone approached Charmaine and offered to buy the house from her for $85,000 cash, she couldn't believe it. With her bad credit and her shaky work history, Charmaine knew she wasn't in any condition to get the home livable or ready to buy another house. And even if she was, $85,000 wouldn't get her the home of her dreams. More like something in the hood that needed a lot of work also. Charmaine decided that she would just take $15,000 of the money to put aside as a down payment when she was ready to buy a house. She'd also buy a new car, get a place and pay the rent up for a year, quit one of her jobs, so she could spend more time with her kids, and go to school online. It all seemed like a great idea to her. But she just didn't want to mess up the only bright spot she had outside of Rico for her future. The last thing Charmaine wanted to do was get the money and blow it and be back broke in a year.

Charmaine knew her mother could be on the money hungry side, so she wasn't telling her about the offer on the sale of the house just yet. She had only been living with her mother for two weeks and Nicole had already hinted around about them leaving twice. Charmaine's kids were kids. They were loud sometimes, and they made messes, and Nicole acted as if the shit just got on her nerves so bad. Charmaine hated being at her mom's house, and if she wasn't smart with the money that she was going to get, she'd be right back depending on her in no time. Charmaine wanted to go on nice trips and stunt like other people her age, but she had kids, and she had to do the right thing with this money. She was tired of struggling. She also had her fingers crossed that everything would go through and that she'd have the check in her hand in the next two weeks or so. Until then, she was going to keep working both her jobs no matter how tired she was. The money would need to last her two years until she could get an associate's degree then start making enough money to buy her and her kids a house. Or by then, hopefully, she wouldn't have to do it alone. The thought of Rico being home to help her made her smile.

"I have a guy coming to look at it tomorrow to see if he can fix it up for me at a reasonable price," Charmaine lied. "Hopefully, me and my kids will be out of here in the next week or so."

Nicole's eyes narrowed as she pulled from the cigarette. "Ummhmmm. I hear you."

When Charmaine was pregnant with her first child, she moved into low income housing where she stayed up until someone broke into her apartment, and she got the hell out of there. Crime had been getting terrible, and she hated having to raise her kids there. Charmaine prayed for a way out every night, and she prayed that this money from the sale of the house would be what she needed to save her. Because her kids' dads didn't help her, all she could afford up until now was an apartment based on income and a ten-year old car that was bound to give out on her any day. She had lost the apartment after the Covid eviction moratorium had expired. Charmaine loved her kids but being a single mother was hard, and it was the reason that she cried damn near every day. For once, she just wanted her luck to turn around.

"If I can't afford to have it fixed, I'll just move in with the mold in the bathroom and pray it doesn't hurt my kids," she stated dryly.

Nicole pushed out a chuckle that turned into a nasty sounding cough. "You can't guilt trip me, lil' girl. I'm not saying you can't stay here, so if you move into a house with mold, that's on you. Your problem is that nobody can't tell you nothing. I tried to tell you them niggas you were running behind wasn't no good, but you didn't want to hear it. I speak from experience, but you had to learn on your own. Now, what I'm simply saying is, I ain't about to raise nor pickup behind no kids. If you can't learn to control them, you just gonna have to be mad at me."

"Yes ma'am," was the reply.

Nicole left out of the kitchen, and Charmaine rolled her eyes again. She couldn't wait to move, there was nothing like having your own shit.

CHARMAINE RAN HER FINGERS THROUGH HER SILKY WEAVE AS SHE waited for Rico to enter the visitation room. She had finally gotten a Saturday off, and she paid her little cousin $50 to watch her kids, so she could drive the hour and a half to see Rico. Charmaine complained about her two jobs, but she'd gotten paid from both jobs Friday and all that overtime from her primary job had her pockets sitting pretty. Charmaine finished up her kid's Christmas shopping, got her hair, nails, and lashes done, and even gave her mom $200. She still had money left, and she was feeling good. Now, what would make the day better was hugging her man.

The door opened, and in walked about five niggas. The best was saved for last because as soon as she saw Rico in the back of the line, a wide smile stretched across her face. Damn her man was fine. Charmaine knew that he might have other women that he was writing to. Maybe he even had other women coming to visit him, but she knew she was special to him. And with all she had going on in her crazy life, she very much so needed to feel special. And Rico made her feel that way. When he approached the table, she stood up, and he gave her just what she needed. A firm bear hug.

"You smell mad good ma," he spoke into her ear and made

her pussy start leaking instantly.

"Thank you," she blushed as he pecked her on the lips.

As soon as they were seated at the table, he grabbed her hand. "You look good as hell. I like your hair like that. Nails all done and shit. I'm glad you got to do something for yourself for a change. You deserve to be able to get that shit done all the time."

"Baby I feel like It's right around the corner. All the being patient and feeling like God wasn't hearing me is paying off. I won't be getting enough to buy a house right now, but I'm going to make sure me and my babies are straight. I can't wait for them to have their own rooms. I want two bathrooms and everything in the guest bathroom will be all white. I've seen the cutest décor on amazon and at Home Goods. I can't wait to decorate babe. Me and my kids are going to live somewhere nice as hell. Maybe a gated apartment community. I'm going to work part-time to have money for utilities, gas money, get Micah's haircut and stuff like that, but I want to be a full-time student. I'm buying a house in the next three years, watch."

"*We're* buying a house in the next three years," Rico corrected her.

Charmaine smiled. "My bad babe. We're buying a house in the next three years. I want the den to have red leather furniture, but I want the living room to be like a crème and silver. I want grey couches and a bunch of blue, silver, and crème décor." There was a far away look in her eyes, and Rico chuckled.

"You love talking about décor."

"That's what I like." Charmaine shook her head. "Too bad I've just been broke as shit and could never afford to execute any of my visions before."

Rico's nostrils flared, and his grip on her hand tightened. "I hate it when you say that. Everyone has been broke before. And like my grandma told me when I came in this bitch. Trouble don't last always. Just hold on. Soon enough, you're going to be living like a queen."

"I can't wait." Charmaine was used to having bad luck, so a part of her was expecting to get a call any day now that something fell through with the house. In the meantime however, she was trying to remain positive. The fact remained that she had access to a home . Even if the sale didn't go through with the company she was working with, Charmaine was sure that someone would buy the home. She simply didn't have the money or the patience to have it fixed up. She absolutely appreciated her grandmother for even leaving her the home. Even though her father wasn't shit, his mother always stepped up to the plate and did for Charmaine be it school shopping or birthday parties.

Candice entered the room and headed over to one of her co-workers. Charmaine glanced up and even though she was far from gay, even she had to do a double take at the woman's ass. "I bet she's popular in here," Charmaine spoke to Rico without taking her eyes off Candice's ample backside.

Rico shrugged passively. "I mean, yeah she is, but it takes more than a fat ass to phase a real nigga. She's eye candy to a bunch of sex deprived inmates. A lot of whom probably weren't even fucking bad bitches in the free world. That shit isn't major to me."

Charmaine nodded. "That makes sense. I wouldn't even want an ass that big. I bet the attention she gets is nuts."

"I've never been an insecure nigga but if your ass was big like that, I'd be bodying niggas left and right. On some real shit, a fat ass on an average chick is just a fat ass. A fat ass on a bad female is a fuckin' problem."

Charmaine giggled even though she knew he was dead serious. She loved it when Rico acted jealous and possessive over her. Damn she couldn't wait for her man to come home! Him being locked up was torture. It had been way too long since she had sex and when he wrote her letters describing the things he'd do to her, she got insanely horny. The couple held hands for the entire visit and talked about everything under the sun. Charmaine was so happy being in Rico's presence and though a lot of people had opinions about her relationship, she refused to believe that things would change when he got home. Nope. They would live happily ever after, and she would finally get her fairy tale.

When the visit was over, Charmaine was sad. But she knew as soon as the check cleared and she put in the two week notice at her job, that she'd have more time to visit Rico. No more mandatory overtime was going to be music to her ears. She was also proud that she was going to give notice like a responsible adult rather than simply telling them to kiss her ass. After Rico and Charmaine stood, he wrapped his arms tightly around her, and they kissed passionately. Their internal timers pulled them apart after about thirty seconds because close contact such as that was against the rules, but the CO's never really tripped as long as they didn't get carried away with it. Charmaine stood in a line at the door with the other visitors. Her nipples were hard, and she had to squeeze her legs together to try and calm the ache in her vagina. At that moment, Charmaine wanted nothing more than to sit on Santa's lap and beg him to bring her man home for Christmas.

"WHAT YOU DOING, GIRL?" JENELLE FLOPPED DOWN BESIDE Charmaine in the breakroom.

"Looking at houses to rent. Being that I have two small kids, I don't know if apartments would be a good idea. I don't want people over my head, but my kids like to run and play. If people are under me, they might complain."

Jenelle nodded in agreement. "I feel you. Rent period is crazy as fuck. If you want to live in a decent area, you're going to get robbed without a gun for either or. I can't wait until I can buy some shit."

"I know right. That's what my man wants to do when he comes home. He wants us to buy a house." Jenelle smirked, and Charmaine became defensive. "What?"

Jenelle held her palms out. "I mean no harm. It's just cute. Listening to all the things a nigga that's locked up has to say. More than ninety percent of them come home and do the exact opposite of what they say they will. A girl can dream though."

Charmaine didn't respond. She bit into a wing and went back to what she was looking at. She hadn't asked Jenelle to sit with her or give her opinion. People always had the most shit to say when they found out she fucked with a man in prison. If Charmaine wanted opinions, she would ask for them. Everyone had something to say about her boyfriend being an inmate. It's not like he was in prison for raping people or killing them. Charmaine's phone vibrated, and she kissed her teeth when she saw who it was. Larry, Micha's father was calling. They broke up when Micah was two months old because he had a gambling problem. He'd leave the house to go buy diapers and end up gambling the money away and coming home empty handed and wanting to take out his frustrations on her. Charmaine got tired of the shit and got rid of him. That infuriated Larry, and he went from only doing for Micah every so often, to not doing for him at all. He was the worst kind of deadbeat there was, and Charmaine hated his ass for it.

"What?" she answered the phone with an attitude. He had a lot of nerve to be calling her. Charmaine hadn't spoken to him in almost five months.

"My mom wants to see Micha on Christmas. Bring him to

her house around three, so he can be around some of my family."

"Fuck you and fuck your mama. I haven't heard from any of you in forever. You missed his birthday, and no one helped me with a fuckin' thing in the past year. Micha doesn't know y'all, and I don't fuck with y'all. He's going to be with my family on Christmas. Period."

"You a dumb bitch. You keep my son away from me because you bitter."

Charmaine let out a loud laugh. "And you're delusional as fuck. If you had anything, I would have taken out child support on you long ago. But I'm not missing work to go to court to hear your bum ass get ordered to pay $50 a month. I'm working two jobs to provide for your son. You don't buy him shit. You go months without calling or texting now I'm the bad guy because I won't take him to your mom. Suck my ass you bitch ass nigga and lose my number."

"You fucking hoe. Everything is always about money, huh? You don't think he wants to spend time with me? Is that even my son? I think we need to do a paternity test."

Charmaine was floored. It had to be crack. This man had to be on serious drugs. There was so much she wanted to say, but she was so stunned, she couldn't even get her mouth to form any of the words, so Charmaine simply ended the call. That man had made so many excuses for being a deadbeat that he actually believed that bull that spewed from his lips. Why would she ever send her son with someone as untrustworthy and irresponsible as him? There were times she felt like she needed a break for sure, but Charmaine would never send her kids with just anybody. And the way they acted, her kids' fathers were just anybody. Kensey's father wasn't any better. Chris had six other kids by five other women, and he wasn't even thirty yet. When Charmaine met him, he only had two other kids. By the time she was seven months pregnant, another woman was expecting a child by him as well. Even Charmaine had to admit to herself that she had some terrible ass luck when it came to men. She chose the wrong ones time and time again, but she prayed with everything in her that this time was different. Only time would tell though.

Chapter
THREE

"Baby, are you sitting down? I got some great news," Rico said into the phone as soon as they were connected. It was two days after their visit, and Charmaine wondered what he sounded so happy about. She had an extremely hard day at work, and she only had two hours to spare before she had to pull a few hours at her part-time job, so she wasn't in the best mood. For her man though, she forced a smile even though he couldn't see her.

"Yes I'm sitting, what's up baby?"

"Yo, so you know my new white boy cellie Joshua. The nigga is Jewish and shit. He been putting me up on game about fucking with this crypto currency trading, investing, and all that. Babe, he showing me how someone invested $50,000 and in less than three months, he had made $185,000 back! That's insane, right?"

"I guess," Charmaine responded slowly. She wanted to

know why he was so excited about that because he for sure didn't have $50,000 to invest.

"You guess? Babe, listen, this man profited $135,000 in three months. That's better than dope money. Imagine what we could do in six months? We could make mad bread then when I come home, I can start driving trucks like I planned, and we'd be set! We could be living in a million dollar house in no time."

Charmaine was starting to get a headache. She didn't know where this we was coming from because to her knowledge, Rico didn't have any money to invest. She knew like hell he wasn't hinting around that he wanted her to invest her money. It sounded good, but she didn't know anything about investing in crypto currency nor did Rico. Just because it worked for someone else didn't mean it would work for her, and she'd be sick to lose that kind of money. Charmaine didn't even want to think about how she'd feel if she were to throw away such a large amount of money based off what someone else said. Her silence made Rico aware that she wasn't with the suggestion, but he continued his pitch anyway.

"Baby. If we give them $50,000 and wait six months, we could have no less than $300,000 I'm sure of it. If we didn't want to wait the whole six and cashed out after three months, that would still get us like $150,000. That's a $100,000 profit. I'm trying to set us up for the long run. Once I come home, I have to spend eight weeks completing truck driving school. A nigga don't want to not have money coming in for two months. This will have us set."

Charmaine didn't want to say what she was thinking for fear that she would piss him off but he wasn't doing anything. It was her money that he wanted her to invest. Once he came home, it would still be her money that they were living off of for two months while he went to school. Charmaine failed to understand what he was actually doing in this scenario for it to be "their" money.

"I don't know, Rico. That's a lot of money, and money like that is hard to come by. What if it doesn't work out? Then me and my kids are out of $50,000 and only left with $35,000 to live off for two years. I'd feel like a complete and utter asshole. I'm not even in a position to take that kind of a gamble."

"Baby, listen to me. I got you. When I say I got you, I mean that shit. I would never let you and the kids be out here without. Not while I'm in prison and not while I'm out there. We're a team, ma. From the moment you became my girl we became a team."

He was talking a good game and any other day, it might be music to Charmaine's ears, but this had her skeptical as hell. She was glad when the automated system alerted them that they only had sixty seconds left. Rico quickly continued his sales pitch, told her he loved her, and said he'd call her back later that night once she left her part-time job. Him asking her to invest $50,000 of her money had truly made Charmaine uncomfortable. She'd never been a selfish person, but she'd also never met the man that she'd take food out of her kids' mouths for. That's where she drew the line. No, $50,000 wouldn't be all of her money. But it would be over half of her money. And that was just too much to risk, even for Rico.

CHARMAINE HAD JUST PULLED UP AT HER MOM'S HOUSE TO GRAB A bite to eat and spend some time with her kids before heading to her other job, when her phone rang. She knew the prison number like the back of her hand, and she almost ignored it because she thought it was Rico calling back. She then remembered that he said he'd call her later, so she answered. It was her cousin calling, and she accepted the call. Tookie was her first cousin, and they were born three months apart. They were more like siblings than cousins.

"Damn bout time you answered, since you got with that nigga, it's been over for my visits," Tookie chuckled. "I'm glad I only have two months left, or I'd be one sad ass nigga."

Charmaine smacked her lips and smiled. "You know it's not even like that. I wish I could visit both of you. With my work schedule, it's been hard even visiting him. How have you been though?"

"I've been good. Can't really complain. Ready to get up out this bitch. But how are you? When I connected you and Rico, I wasn't really sure how far it would go, but it's been a lil' minute. You really like this nigga?"

"I do. He's a really good person. I mean, that's what I honestly feel." Charmaine had to stop herself from going to bat for Rico. It wasn't like Tookie didn't know him. Tookie knew him better than she did. It would be quite embarrassing if she was going hard for a person that had already shown his true colors to Tookie. But then again, why would he turn her on to someone that wasn't shit?

"I can't say what he is and what he isn't. He has pictures of you and him in his pod. I've never seen any other females on his wall. I haven't heard of any females coming to visit him, but I'd be a shitty ass big cousin if I didn't tell you to be careful. A lot of men in here find women to latch onto before it's time for them to come home. They write some sweet letters, kick some good game on the phone then boom, they come home to automatic in house pussy. They have a furnished crib to lay their head in, and life is great until some of them get on their feet, and their true colors begin to show. Dude is in this bitch for scamming. So just be careful."

Charmaine bit her bottom lip. She had kept it quiet from everyone that she was selling the house that her grandmother left to her. Really, Rico was the only person that knew. So, was Tookie telling her this some kind of sign? Was God trying to tell her to go with her gut and not give Rico the $50,000 he was requesting? She would give him a place to live when he came home. In house pussy, home cooked meals, she'd even be patient while he finished trucking school. She'd rather do all that then to just sign over $50,000 on something neither one of them really knew about.

"I will, but I don't think he'd do me like that though. I don't have anything for him to scam," she laughed lightly while her stomach churned.

Tookie laughed, "Cuzzo never underestimate shit. Rico was a top tier scammer. Nigga was getting credit cards with $50,000 limits. He was getting females to cash fake checks and all that shit. The house that he stayed in, the furniture was even in someone else's name. He would go into any store that gave credit and open up a line using a fake ID and a social security number. He lived the fucking good life for a few years before he got knocked, word."

Charmaine's headache started getting worse. She dreaded having to go to work because she had too much on her mind. Everything had been going good with her and Rico and now this. That was the main reason she had decided to keep the news from everyone else, but what was the point of having a significant other if you couldn't share important things with them? Charmaine switched the subject, and her and Tookie talked until time ran out. When her phone rang again, Charmaine screamed.

"Hello?" she answered while trying to hide the agitation that she was feeling.

"Hi. May I speak to Charmaine Knowles?"

"Speaking," Charmaine's tone changed at the sound of the perky sounding white woman.

"Hi. This is Amber from Blake Realty. I just wanted to let you know that your check is ready for pickup."

A wide smile stretched across her face. "Thank you. I'll be

by to get it shortly. It looked like Charmaine would be calling in to her part-time job today.

"WORKING ALL THOSE HOURS MUST BE PAYING OFF," NICOLE peered over at her daughter while Charmaine wrapped the last of the gifts that she got for her kids. There were more than twenty presents under the tree. Charmaine was happy she had gotten her kids all the things that they wanted and then some.

"Yeah they have been." Charmaine had been in an excellent mood since depositing that check into her bank account. She was going to wait until her two weeks at work were up. Once she was no longer working during the day, she'd go look for a place for her and her kids to live, then she'd get a car. Charmaine didn't want to pull up to her mother's house in a new car. And she didn't plan on telling her mother that she was quitting her job.

"Well, the kids will be happy, but remember that Christmas comes once a year. You still have to live after that."

Charmaine bit her tongue, so she wouldn't be disrespectful. She didn't understand why her mother couldn't just let her have this moment. Charmaine just wanted to make her kids happy. She didn't need lectures from her mother. Her and her kids were straight. Her phone rang, and Charmaine saw that Rico was calling her. With a big smile, she answered the phone. "Hey babe," she greeted him once they were connected. "I got the money. Thank you. You didn't have to do that."

Earlier, someone had sent her a cash app for $150 with a note saying it was from Rico. He didn't know that she'd gotten her check, and he kept his word and made sure she got some money. After that, Charmaine felt less uneasy about trusting him. Rico was a good man, and he loved her. No one could tell her otherwise.

"You don't have to thank me for that. I'm your man, and the holidays are coming up. I honestly wish I could do more. You know how it kills me that I can't go shopping for you? I'd love to see the smile on your face when I come in the house with big bags and shit."

Charmaine bit her bottom lip and blushed. Rico had a way of making her feel a way that no other man ever had before. Not even her two baby daddies. "Well, you'll be here soon enough. Our first Christmas together will be an awesome one."

"I can't wait. Listen, babe. My cellie gave me the information of a woman by the name of Lauren. She's one of the investors that can walk you through the process of investing the money. She can meet with you and answer any questions that you have. That way, you can see that this is legit, and you have nothing to worry about. All you have to do is call her and set up a time to meet. That's it. You don't have to have the money to meet with her."

Charmaine blew out a shaky breath. They were back on the $50,000. She thought about how Rico was in prison, and on two separate occasions, he'd given her money when he could have been keeping it for himself. Rico had never asked her for a thing. Every time he called her the calls were prepaid. She never once put money on his books, and he never asked her to. Up until a month ago, he didn't even know she was going to sell her grandmother's house and get any money. What could he have been using her for?

"Sure. Give me the number. I'll talk to her and see what she has to say."

That seemed to excite Rico. He was elated that she had agreed to contact Lauren. Once their fifteen minutes were up, the call ended, and Nicole appeared in the room out of nowhere. "You still talking to that jailbird, huh? Just be careful because those inmates are slicker than hen piss. They'll tell you anything. You've already been through it twice with two slick niggas. Don't get caught up with a third."

Charmaine wanted to give Nicole a piece of her mind, but once again, she remained silent. Everything she did, her mother found something wrong with it. Charmaine couldn't wait to move the hell up out of her mother's house.

"I HEARD YOU'RE ONE OF THE ONES LEAVING," CANDICE ENTERED Rico's pod while he was packing his things up.

He looked over at her. They spoke on a cordial level sometimes. It wasn't too often. A lot of the inmates gassed her because of her ass but in prison or not, Rico wasn't about to be acting like a groupie. "Yeap. I'm getting the hell up out of here. Tomorrow can't come fast enough."

"Well stay out of trouble. I don't want to see you back in here."

"Copy that."

Candice lingered like there was more that she wanted to say. Rico didn't speak. He continued to sort through his things. Very little of it was going home with him. What he didn't throw in the trash, he would give to other inmates.

"Seeing as how you're about to get out, I wanted to give you my number. I'd never risk my job dealing with an inmate, but once you're on the street, you're fair game."

Rico looked over at Candice and was astonished to find her looking him up and down like she wanted to pounce on him at that very moment. He chuckled inwardly. Wasn't this some shit? She often tried to act offended and mad at the inmates that cracked on her. And the entire time, she'd been sizing him up. He could respect the fact that she wasn't about to risk her job for him. He saw correctional officers get fired every day for giving inmates special privileges, bringing in contraband, and having relationships with them. Rico walked over to his desk and picked up a notebook and a pen. Candice quickly wrote her number down and scurried out of his pod.

Rico stared at the number with a smirk on his face. He was going home to Charmaine, but he never knew when he might need a friend on the outside. Especially with the way Charmaine was starting to act since getting the check. Also he wasn't about to risk pissing Candice off if he rejected her. He didn't need to have a bitter CO handling him so close to being released.

Chapter FOUR

Charmaine walked inside the office with raised brows as her eyes swept over the white woman that stood before her with a big smile on her face. She was indeed Caucasian, but she had the body of a black woman. In fact, her body put Charmaine's to shame. She had the smallest waist and the fattest ass that Charmaine had ever seen on a white girl. Her skin was tanned, and she had on long dramatic lashes, a face full of make-up, and Charmaine could tell that she'd gotten her lips done. Long jet-black hair hung down to her ass, and she was clad in a red wrap dress that hugged her frame. On her feet were black, pointy toe Louboutin heels. Ole girl looked like a real life Bratz doll. She was freaking gorgeous.

"Hi, I'm looking for Lauren."

"Yes, I'm Lauren, and you must be Charmaine! Rico is so excited that we're meeting today. I talked to him this morning,"

Lauren extended her hand for Charmaine to shake. Meanwhile, Charmaine's stomach caved in.

It was something about the way Lauren said Rico's name that made her feel some kind of way. They had been talking on the phone? Of course, Rico couldn't see her through the phone, but Charmaine was slightly intimidated. Why? She didn't really know, but she eyed the diamond ring on Lauren's finger. It wasn't an engagement ring because it was on her right hand. The smell of the expensive perfume that she was wearing smelled like money. She seemed like the kind of boss bitch that Rico would love. Charmaine wasn't sure why she was being so insecure all of a sudden, and she shook her worries off.

"It's nice to meet you. And yes, Rico is very excited. Which is why I'm here."

Lauren pointed to a chair. "Well let's get down to business. I'd be more than happy to answer any questions that you may have. Once we're done, you take all the time you need to figure out what you want to do, but I have to be honest with you. The Crypto market can be a finnicky thing. When something is hot and making money, you want to strike while the iron is hot. If you do that and know the in's and outs, you can invest, cash out in a few months, and enjoy your profit before the heat dies down."

Charmaine sat down and took in everything that Lauren was saying. She seemed to be very knowledgeable on Crypto stocks and investing. She said there was no guarantee, but she also pretty much assured Charmaine that she could turn her $50,000 into $300,000 in three months tops. Charmaine was still nervous about letting that kind of money go, but she listened to Lauren talk for almost twenty minutes. Lauren showed her portfolios of money that she had made other clients, and Charmaine's eyes ballooned out when she saw that someone had cashed out $400,000 earlier that day. Lauren stated that he had been investing his money with her for five years, and he only started with $1,600. That was impressive as hell to her.

Lauren really had the gift of gab, and she had convinced Charmaine to open an account and transfer $50,000 of her money into the account for Lauren to invest. When she left the office, Charmaine's nerves were so bad that her palms wouldn't stop sweating. Even though Lauren had given a good sales pitch, and she knew Rico would be so happy. Charmaine was still nervous about letting go of that kind of money. All she could do was hope that it didn't come back to bite her in the ass.

LATER THAT DAY, RICO CALLED CHARMAINE WHILE SHE WAS picking her kids up from daycare. As soon as their call connected, she made him aware that she had met with Lauren. "Or did she already tell you? I wasn't aware that you've had phone conversations with her."

"Umm yeah. I needed to see where her head was at before I even turned you on to her. It's your money, but I meant what I said when I said we're a team. I'm not about to let you give your money to some bullshit. I love you and the kids too much to risk that. Again I got us in any way that I can."

The conviction in his voice made Charmaine feel bad for being jealous. She was jealous of a female that Rico couldn't even see. And truthfully, the only things she really had on Charmaine were a fat ass, flat stomach, and money. Charmaine wasn't broke any more herself and even though she had a little pudge, it never stopped anything with Rico. She knew for a fact that her man was attracted to her even with her muffin top and all.

"I appreciate that. She really seemed to know her shit. I just pray that nothing goes wrong."

"Baby, stop stressing. Everything's coming together for us. I have some wonderful news that I was holding until the right time. I need you to call out of work tomorrow."

Charmaine frowned up her face. "Why?" Even though she only had five more days to work, she still wasn't sure about calling out. Being that she had two kids, she never knew when one of them would get sick, so calling out of work for bullshit had never been her thing.

"I just got the final word, that due to all the covid cases, fifty non-violent offenders were granted early release, and I was one of them. I need you to pick me up tomorrow at noon."

Charmaine gasped. "You're fucking lying! Babe, are you for real?" Charmaine was so happy it felt like her heart was about to burst out of her chest. It was pumping hard as hell. She was holding her breath while she waited on Rico to answer. If he was playing with her, she just might hang up on his ass.

He chuckled. "I'm dead ass serious. I damn near had a heart attack when they told me that shit. There's like fifty cases of covid in here among inmates, and there have been five deaths in the past month. They're doing whatever they can to try and help the cause, and I'm not mad at them. I haven't had any infractions in a year and some change, I'm not in here for a violent crime, and I'll just be on probation for a year. I have to take weekly drug tests and show proof that I'm looking for a job. But that's it I'm out of here"

"I can't believe this!" Charmaine screamed so loud her kids were looking at her like she was crazy. "This is the best Christmas present ever." She looked down at her nails happy that she had already gotten them done and a pedicure. If she couldn't find anyone to fit her in for a wax appointment on such short notice, she would shave. But Charmaine loved how smooth, pretty, and soft her pussy was after a fresh wax. It hurt like a bitch, but the results were worth it. Being that she'd been celibate for so long and broke, it had been a while since she got waxed, but this was a very special occasion.

"I know, baby. I'm happy as hell. My dick is hard just thinking about the fact that you're going to be in my arms in less than twenty-four hours."

Charmaine was so excited she didn't know what to do with herself. She took the kids to get happy meals while her and Rico made plans over the phone. When they got off the phone, she headed to the mall to grab him some boxers, socks, shoes, and a fly outfit for him to come home in. She even bought him a coat and some cologne. After shopping, she took the kids home to her mother and asked her to baby-sit while she went to her part-time job. Charmaine didn't really have to work. She wanted to go get a Brazilian wax. She then went online and reserved a hotel suite that set her back almost $300, but she didn't give a damn. This was a special occasion.

Charmaine went and got everything that she would need in order to make the day with Rico a special one. She would have about five and a half hours with him before she had to pick her kids up from daycare, and she planned to make it count. Now, Charmaine was really irritated with herself that she hadn't already found a place to live. That way, she could spend the entire night with him. She wondered where he would live until she got a place. Maybe he'd stay with his mom. Charmaine left everything she got him in the car when she went in for the night. She was so excited she could barely sleep. Her nigga was on his way home!

THE NEXT DAY, CHARMAINE RAN AND JUMPED INTO RICO'S ARMS so damn fast she almost knocked him down. All he could do was laugh and wrap his arms around her. It felt damn good to have a woman that excited for him to be coming home. The fact that he knew very soon he'd be in some pussy had him happy as hell also. But nothing was better than freedom. Rico inhaled hard as if he'd never smelled fresh air before. Charmaine felt so good in his arms, but he wanted to get away from the prison ASAP. "Let's go," he tapped her on the ass and placed her feet on the ground.

"You want to drive?" she asked him. Charmaine knew that Rico didn't give a damn what he came home in, but she wished she had more time to get herself together before his release. She wished she already had a home and a new car, but her raggedy one would have to do for now.

"Yeah. I'll drive."

Charmaine handed him the keys and bit her bottom lip lustfully as she eyed his muscular arms. Got damn this man was fine! He looked like he could bench press her easy as hell even with the few extra pounds that she had put on. Once they were in the car, Rico looked over at her. "You know I gotta stay in the halfway house, right? I can't just come home."

Charmaine pouted. "Oh. I didn't know that. Where is the halfway house?"

"I have the address with my things. We're not even allowed to have cellphones in that bitch, but my people gonna sneak me one in. Like a nigga gon' be up in that joint with no phone. Still, bullshit aside, I'm happy to be free. I have to report there by five."

Charmaine was disappointed, but some time with him was better than no time. "That's cool. I guess we should go straight to the hotel then."

"Oh word, you got a room? That's what's up. I want to go holla at Lauren first though. I know we have to give the shit some time to work, but I'm anxious. I need her to show a nigga what she can do for real."

Charmaine swallowed hard. Why did he want to go see Lauren with her huge ass? Charmaine had to attribute her low self-esteem to her not shit baby daddies that would get mad and talk to her any kind of way. They cheated and made her feel less than, plenty of times. Micah's dad, Rod even had a way of making her feel like she wasn't good enough for him, and he didn't even have shit. It was weird the way she let them get into her head, but she had. She refused to show Rico just how insecure she was though. He put the address of the office into her GPS and began the drive there.

"You can leave the halfway house sometimes, right? I want us to go look at places when I get off tomorrow. That way when you leave there, you can come home to me and the kids like we planned."

Rico looked over at her. "I have to be in the halfway house for three months. I know you might not want to, but I think we should hold off on getting a place until then. By that time, Lauren will have flipped the money, and we can get a house. Why rent with all the money we about to be sitting on?"

Lauren stared out of the window. Yes, they were a team, but there he went with that we shit again. So far, she was the only one forking over money. And she simply refused to live with her mother for three more months. Maybe she could find a place that would let her do a six month lease. Rather than telling him that, she decided to just go behind his back and do it. Afterall, it was her money. She didn't need his opinion or his approval. It took them an hour and ten minutes to get from the prison to Lauren's office. When they entered, Charmaine saw how Lauren's eyes lit up when she saw Rico.

"Yo. I'm Rico. They let a nigga out early, so I came by to see how that's going. And I know it's very soon. I just want to talk to you in person. Now, we're not restricted by that fifteen minutes."

Lauren stood up with that big ass grin on her face, and Charmaine could tell that she wasn't going to like this meeting. Lauren walked around the desk, and Charmaine could see that she was clad in a black skirt, a red sweater, and black thigh high boots. Her ass looked even bigger than it had the first time Charmaine saw her, and she knew Rico noticed it too. As usual, Lauren smelled good as hell, and she was on point from head to toe. Charmaine even noticed an iced out watch on her wrist and wondered if it had been there the first time they met.

"Damn you all icy," Rico joked. He was being friendly, but Charmaine perceived it as flirting. She bit her tongue though. It might not be smart to piss off a person that had $50,000 of her money.

"And if ice is your thing, you'll be even icier in no time," Lauren smiled and walked back to her desk.

The nerve of her. How in the hell was Rico going to be icy when it was Charmaine's money that was invested? Did they look at her as some kind of a joke? Charmaine sat down beside Rico and listened as Lauren went over the same things with Rico that she had with her. It just didn't sit well with Charmaine that Lauren and Rico were in such a deep discussion over *her* money. Rico looked excited as hell and was rubbing his hands together anxiously. Charmaine appreciated him for looking out for her and if this did work out, then Rico could reap the benefits of living with her in her house. He could have access to her car. She would even pay for him to go to truck driving school, but she wasn't putting any money in his hands directly. Not for him to decide that he wanted to take her money and go trick on the next bitch. Charmaine didn't like the thoughts that she was having, but they were at the forefront of her mind.

When Lauren was done going over everything, Rico shook her hand, and they stood up to leave. "Yo I told you shorty was about her shit," he said all hype and shit when they got in the car.

Charmaine turned towards him with a slight scowl on her

face. "She can tell you anything. We can't be for sure she's about her shit until I make some real money back."

"It's going to happen in due time, babe. You just have to be patient."

Charmaine remained quiet as Rico drove towards the hotel. She didn't want to spend his first day home in her feelings. She was tripping, and she needed to get over the shit. Once they arrived at the hotel, and he shut off the car, Charmaine asked him to pop the trunk. When he did so, she walked to the back of the car and grabbed the many bags. "What's all this?" Rico asked as he eyed the bags.

"A surprise."

They entered the lobby, so she could check in. Rico looked around the hotel lobby in awe. Of course, he had been in nice hotels before. He used to commit credit card fraud. Rico only ate the finest food, wore the finest clothes, drank the finest liquor, smoked the finest weed, and slept in the most luxurious places when he was doing his dirt. And though he knew Charmaine wasn't broke, he was still kind of shocked that she had gone all out for him. The desk attendant handed Charmaine the key, and they walked to the elevator. She was glad they had a room on the tenth floor. Even though it wasn't dark out yet, they would still have a pretty awesome view of the city. In the elevator, Rico stood behind Charmaine, wrapped his arms around her, and nuzzled his face in the crook of her neck. "This is nice as hell, babe. Thank you."

It felt so good being in his arms that Charmaine almost moaned. "Thank you, and it's only going to get better."

The elevator reached their floor, and Charmaine's mouth became dry as she looked for the room. She really couldn't believe that the moment she'd been dreaming about for a year was coming true. She was nervous, excited, and anxious. All of the different emotions she was feeling had her feeling like she would throw up any minute. Charmaine had gone all out and bought a $160 bottle of Don Julio that she couldn't wait to get her hands on. There was no way she could relax completely sober. She had known Rico for a year, but she'd never been alone with him before. It was almost like he was a stranger.

When they entered the room, Charmaine handed him three of the bags. "You can go take a shower if you want. I got you boxers, socks, shoes, an outfit, cologne, and a toothbrush. I even got you deodorant. And," she placed the rest of the bags on the bed and picked up a bottle of henny from her bag. "I got us this, so we can relax."

Rico smiled. "You damn sure know how to welcome a nigga home." He cupped her chin in his hand and tongued her down. He kissed her passionately and aggressively. The way he never could in the visitation room at the prison. Rico kissed Charmaine with so much passion, that her pussy began leaking like a faucet. She'd never been kissed like that in her life and when he started sucking on her tongue, she moaned. She hoped he would take the quickest shower ever. All Charmaine wanted was Rico inside of her. Fuck everything else.

He pulled back with a devilish grin and smacked her hard on the ass. "Be ready for me when I get out of the shower. I'm talking butt ass naked."

As soon as he shut the bathroom door behind him, Charmaine grabbed the room key and found the ice machine. Back in the room, she pulled a Coke from her bag of goodies, and placed some ice in a cup. There was no way she could drink the Hennessey straight. Charmaine fixed a drink that was one part liquor and two parts soda. After taking several sips, her body felt warm, and she was more ready to have sex than she'd ever been. Charmaine sprinkled rose petals all over the floor and the bed and lit some candles. She hurriedly stripped out of her clothes and put on the black, lace, see-through teddy that was in her bag.

Charmaine was sipping on her second drink when she

heard the shower water turn off. She was as giddy as a kid on Christmas about to open their gifts. When Rico opened the bathroom door naked as hell with steam wafting out of the bathroom behind him, Charmaine's mouth fell open from the sight before her. His chiseled body and that dick. Baby, that dick was hard as hell and pointed straight at her. Charmaine's mouth was watering for it so much so, that she walked over to him and dropped down to her knees.

"Yes baby," Rico moaned as she took him into her mouth. She took him in slowly knowing she wouldn't be able to fit all of him in there, but she had to try. Charmaine wanted to bring him as much pleasure as she hoped he was going to bring her. She almost had him in when she gagged.

Charmaine began to move her head up and down slowly. Rico placed one hand firmly on the back of her head, and she sped up the speed at which she was sucking his dick. Charmaine pulled back and spit on his dick, and Rico moaned loud as hell. "That's what I'm talking about baby." He began thrusting his hips and fucking her mouth.

Just as a tear spilled over Charmaine's eyelid, Rico released a guttural moan as he released into her mouth. "I need that muhfuckin' pussy," he grunted as she stood up.

Charmaine lay flat on her back because she wanted to look up into her man's face as he stroked her. This was the start of their new beginning together, and she was thrilled. All of the answers to her prayers seemed to be coming true. She was able to give her kids a great Christmas, she would no longer have to give up spending time with them to work sixty hours a week, and she now had a man. And not only did she have a man, but she had a good man. After taking so many losses, she finally felt like she was winning, and it felt damn good.

"Damn this shit tight and wet," Rico sighed as he slowly pushed into her inch by inch. Women could be some good ass liars, but he really believed she hadn't been giving up the goods. She was wet as hell, and it still took him some time to work his way into her. That shit was really impressive considering she had two kids. Rico wasn't sure why niggas always thought women with kids had loose pussies. That shit was far from true for the majority of them and Charmaine was proving that.

"Rico, you feel so good, baby. This is what I've been waiting for," tears filled Charmaine's eyes as Rico fucked her hard and fast.

"That shit feels good mami?" he peered into her face, and she nodded her head feverishly.

Rico pulled out of her and placed his face between her legs. His tongue circled around her clit before he stiffened it and stuck the tip inside her center. Charmaine went crazy. Her body jerked as she locked her legs around his neck damn near suffocating him.

That didn't stop him from spreading her pussy open and devouring her clit until she was screaming his name and creaming on his tongue. Rico knew that if there was anybody in the next room they probably heard her, but he damn sure didn't care. When he eased back into her, he moaned pretty loud his damn self. He had missed pussy something terrible. Rico hit Charmaine with a few deep strokes then pulled out of her. "Let me get this shit from the back." He spoke while turning her over.

Charmaine got on all fours, and Rico penetrated her from behind. Five minutes later, he was releasing his semen onto her ass cheeks even though she was on birth control. He wasn't really trying to take any chances. He knew he was backed up terribly, and his sperm were probably strong as hell. A baby wasn't what he needed at the moment, and he knew Charmaine for sure didn't need another one right now. Rico's mouth was dry, so he eased off the bed and fixed some Hennessey with ice while Charmaine lay there staring at his sexy, sweaty, naked body.

"Just give me like five minutes, and we're going for round two," he promised. All Charmaine could do was smile. Her body was limp, and she was satisfied. Charmaine didn't want to miss a moment with Rico, so sleep wasn't an option. She knew once she got him to the halfway house, got home and showered, that she'd sleep like a baby for the rest of the night.

Four hours later, Rico had busted three nuts, and Charmaine was dropping him off at the halfway house. Her pussy was sore, and her thighs were aching, but pain had never felt so good. Her body had been worked out in a way that it hadn't been in years. Her legs were so weak, she didn't even want to get out of the car to hug Rico. He leaned over the armrest and kissed her on the lips. "I'm going to hit you up later, okay? My people's is going to sneak me a phone up in here."

"Please don't get in trouble," Charmaine pleaded.

"Babe, I'm not. I got this. Go home and get some sleep. You look tired," he smirked knowing he had worn her out.

Charmaine grinned lazily. "I most certainly am. As soon as I get my kids to bed. I love you."

"I love you too. You held a nigga down, and I won't ever forget that." Time was of the essence, so he kissed her again and got out of the car.

Charmaine made sure he made it safely inside and once she drove off, she screamed loud as hell. "My man is home!"

Chapter FIVE

"I thought you were done shopping, babe," Rico stated as he and Charmaine walked through the mall. They had just left Target. He had been walking in behind her all morning while she shopped.

"I was done with the kids. I have to get my mom some stuff, my aunt, and my grandma. Plus, we did Secret Santa at work. I'll get your gift when I'm not with you." She winked at him.

"I can't tell you were done with the kids, because I know those toys you got in Target weren't for your mom, your aunt, or your co-worker," he chuckled. "And you don't have to get me anything, ma. You've done enough."

Charmaine heard what he said, but she still planned to get him something. This was the first Christmas in a few years that she wasn't stressed out that she couldn't go all out for her kids. Charmaine didn't care what anyone said. She wanted her kids to love Christmas and not grow up with stories about how their mother could never afford to get them nice gifts. Charmaine vowed next Christmas to pick a name off the Angel tree in the mall and to go shopping for someone else's child. That would really make her feel good.

"What do you want for Christmas?" he asked her as they walked through the crowded mall.

"I have everything I want for Christmas." Charmaine knew that he was just coming home, and he didn't have the money to get anyone a gift for Christmas, and she didn't mind at all. One thing she felt for sure, was that if Rico had the money, he would have spoiled her something serious for Christmas. She knew he liked nice things, and she was proud that he wasn't risking his freedom by committing some type of fraud to buy things. Hopefully, prison had taught him a lesson about that. Fast money often wasn't worth it. That thought reminded her about the money that she gave Lauren, and she began to feel uneasy. Lord, please don't let Lauren mess her over and screw her out of $50,000.

"Okay, but if you could get one thing. Anything in the world. What would it be?"

It didn't take Charmaine long to answer that question. "A fully loaded Range Rover for sure. I have a little money, but I'm not cashing out like that just yet. I'll probably get a Camry or something sensible for now but as soon as I get on my feet, I'm coming for that Range."

Charmaine was super thankful for the money she got from selling the house, but she was far from rich. To cash out on a Range Rover would take a huge portion of her money and even if she made monthly payments, they were sure to be high as hell. The car payments along with the maintenance on a luxury vehicle wasn't something she was sure she was ready for at the time, but that was okay. Charmaine knew that in due time she would get everything that she wanted. Many nights, she prayed just to be able to live comfortably without working herself to death or stressing all the time, and God had made that possible for her. She also prayed for a good man time and time again, and God had made that happen for her too. Now, Charmaine truly had everything that she wanted, and she couldn't be happier. As if he could read her mind, Rico inched closer to her and wrapped his arm around her neck as they made their way out of the mall. Yes, for once in her life, everything was going right for Charmaine.

THE NEXT DAY WHEN CHARMAINE GOT OFF WORK, SHE HURRIED to the hotel, so she could get a room for her and Rico. She gave up on dwelling on the fact that she wouldn't be wasting money on a hotel if she had her own place. This room wasn't as lavish as the one he came home to because they would only be there for a few hours. Charmaine was off from her part-time job, but that didn't mean anything. Rico had to report back to the halfway house by a certain time. She had to remind herself that it was only temporary. She was tempted to just go ahead and quit her job, so she could spend her days with him, but she decided against it. She only had a few more days left anyway. Surly she could hold out for that long.

After she got the key to the room, Charmaine headed to pick Rico up. When he was walking out to the car dressed in grey sweats, a white shirt, black sneakers, and the black coat she bought him, all Charmaine could do was smile. He was so damn fine, and he was all hers. When he got in the car, he leaned over and kissed her on the lips. His eyes then roamed over her body. "You look good babe."

Charmaine blushed. "Thank you. You want to go get something to eat?"

Rico sat back and rubbed his stomach. "Fuck yes. I'm

hungry as hell. Take me to Bojangles. I've been craving the fuck out of their fries."

"Okay." It was little things like being able to take Rico to get food that made her feel good. Him coming home happened so abruptly, that it still didn't seem real. Charmaine went from being stressed and lonely to having her man by her side. Soon, she would no longer have to work like a slave, and she could focus on bettering herself and her kids.

After they got the food and went to the hotel room, Rico devoured his order in less than fifteen minutes. When his belly was good and full, he devoured Charmaine. In the hour that he kissed, licked, sucked on, and stroked her, she had three orgasms. Rico intertwined his fingers with hers, licked his lips, and stared into her eyes as they lay in bed after their love making session ended.

"You have a boy and a girl. So, what do you want your next child to be?"

"I thought I was done after my daughter, so I haven't really thought about it. Since I have one of each, the gender of the next one wouldn't really matter to me. If I had to choose though, I'd say a boy. When girls start wanting their hair done and nails and all that, they get expensive. What about you?"

"I want a son first and then a daughter. And my daughter isn't wearing all that weave and getting her nails and shit done until she's in high school. My shorty won't be in middle school wearing fake lashes and shit. One of the reasons I want my son first, is so we can fuck niggas up behind his sister."

Charmaine giggled. She loved the idea of a father being overprotective and very active in his daughter's life. Just like that, Charmaine had gone from swearing off more kids to being willing to give Rico kids if that's what he wanted. Thinking back to her conversation with Larry, she knew that she'd never have to worry about that with Rico. She knew he would be an excellent father.

"When are you thinking about enrolling in truck driving school?"

"I'm going to talk to the guy next week. I'm ready to get something cracking because being in that halfway house during the day isn't hitting on shit. I hate that funky ass house. It's almost like being back in prison. But at least a nigga is free though."

Charmaine rubbed his muscular arm in an effort to comfort him. She was ready for Rico to have everything he wanted. He deserved it. Charmaine felt something poking in her side, and she had to smile knowing that Rico's dick had gotten back hard. He couldn't get enough of her, and the feeling was mutual. She straddled him, and round two of sex started. When they were done, it was time for him to get back to the halfway house. He was in the bathroom cleaning up, and his phone vibrated on the nightstand. Charmaine glanced over at it and saw the letters, LM. Her eyes shifted towards the bathroom, and she wondered who LM was. Maybe it was a guy. Or maybe it was a female. Charmaine hated being jealous, but she'd been through too much to just trust a nigga because he claimed he was a good one.

The phone stopped ringing and just as she was about to tear her eyes away from the screen, a text message from LM came through. *Hit me back ASAP.* What made Charmaine mad was the emoji that came after that. It was the emoji that was smirking. The one that had the look that you text someone when you just said some slick shit or when you're thinking some slick shit. That's not an emoji that a man would be sending another man. Charmaine didn't want to beef with Rico, but she wasn't about to bite her tongue and let shit slide for the sake of keeping the peace. He was her nigga, right? So she should be able to ask who was calling and texting him. Rico entered the room brushing his waves.

"Baby, LM called you then texted you. Who is that?" she asked casually.

Rico walked over to the phone and looked at it without answering her. That pissed her off because it made her feel like he was looking for clues. Had he said it was nigga, she could argue the fact that the emoji was one a female would have sent him. "Did you not hear what I just asked you?" she remained calm.

"Chill. It's about business. Don't start tripping babe."

Charmaine wasn't sure how to take it. She didn't want to nag him, but she didn't want to be stupid either. Was he talking to other women? As he gathered his things so they could leave the room, she did the same thing. Charmaine took a deep breath and decided to just let the shit go. For now. God help Rico if he was being foul. She didn't have it in her to take being done wrong by another man.

"CAN I USE YOUR CAR WHILE YOU'RE AT WORK TOMORROW, BABE? I want to complete some job applications in person. Talk to a manager or something. I don't like all this online shit then waiting to hear back. Most times, I be forgetting to check my email."

"Yeah, you can use my car tomorrow. Just please make sure you're back by five to pick me up. And not a minute later. Traffic is mad thick around that time, and I have to get my kids from daycare by six."

"I'll be done way before six. I plan to be done by noon. You know what they say. The early bird gets the worm. I'm not out here playing."

Charmaine smiled. Rico had been home for six days, and it had been great. They had done a lot of fucking. So much that Charmaine wasn't even mad when her period came on that morning. She needed a small break, because Rico's sex drive was insane.

"I also want to holla at Lauren too," he stated, and Charmaine blew out a small breath. Rico noticed the less than pleased look on her face. "What's good? Why you looking at me like that?"

Charmaine wasn't trying to start an argument, but she wasn't about to keep biting her tongue. "You said yourself that this takes at least a month or two to even see a little profit. Lauren hasn't even had the money for two weeks, and you've already talked to her several times. Why do you need to keep talking to her? You're acting more anxious than me, and it's my money. I mean, how is she talking to you so freely about everything when it's *my* money? I don't understand that."

Rico chuckled. "Damn, let's make no mistake about it. That's definitely *your* money, and I'm not trying to take that from you lil' mama. Lauren feels like it's cool to discuss the money with me because she assumes we're a team. Just like I did, but you're right. It's your money. I won't say anything else about it. You can go ahead and take me back to the halfway house."

He was mad, and Charmaine felt like shit. She stared at him for a moment and even after she opened her mouth, no words came out. She cleared her throat and tried again. "I'm sorry, Rico. I didn't mean it like that."

He stared out of the window and didn't look at her as he spoke. "You said exactly what you meant, and you let me know how you feel. It is what it is, ma."

Now, she would have to admit that she was insecure if she wanted to look like a decent person even a little bit. "Rico, it's not just the money. Lauren is a beautiful woman. She's classy and well put together. Her body is amazing. And I saw her flirting with you right in my face. I just don't like when you're around her. It might sound stupid, but it's how I feel."

Rico turned to look at her. "That woman was not flirting with me. She was trying to make us comfortable because she has a shit load of money in her possession that belongs to you, and she wanted to make us feel good about it. Yeah, she is pretty, but what does that mean? If it's one thing I learned in prison, it was discipline. I don't have to stick my dick in every female that looks decent. I don't even want you being insecure about that shit, but I'm kind of tight right now, I'm not even gon' lie. I saw that folder in the backseat. You're out looking for apartments even after I asked you to wait. You don't give a damn about what I have to say, huh?"

"That's not true," Charmaine protested. "I respect your opinion, but you're not the one that has to live with my mother. I can't stay there for another three months, and the home buying process isn't a quick one. I've been looking at places that offer six-month leases. That way, by the time the lease is up, we should have our home."

"It doesn't even matter now, because I definitely feel like we should hold off on that. I don't want us to get a house with the money that Lauren makes you. I want to wait until I'm done with truck driving school. That way, I can get a job and contribute. I don't want to be laid up in the crib every day with you walking through reminding me that it's your shit."

Charmaine's heart sank. "Rico, please stop acting like this. I was being weird for a second, and I'm sorry. Even when you didn't have a lot, you've always been good to me. We are a team, and I mean that from the bottom of my heart."

Rico appeared to be calming down a bit, but he didn't say anything. Charmaine reached over and grabbed his hand. "I'm not taking you back to the halfway house until I know for a fact that you're not mad with me anymore." She gazed at him with a pleading look in her eyes.

Rico turned to face her. "We're good, baby." He leaned over and kissed her on the lips. Charmaine stared into his face trying to find clues that he really wasn't upset anymore. The last thing she wanted was for Rico to be mad with her. Not over money even if it was a large amount of cash. She wouldn't be happy to have the money and not have him, so she knew she needed to get it together.

Chapter SIX

"**A**ppreciate you, fam. I'll hit you up later." Rico gave one of his homies dap and headed for Charmaine's car. He had bullshitted a little bit with one of his friends. They shopped a little bit, smoked a blunt, went and got some food, and now they were parting ways. Rico needed to go meet with Lauren.

Charmaine didn't know it, but Rico and Lauren had business prior to him getting Charmaine to invest money with the company that Lauren worked for. Charmaine didn't need to know their history, so Rico kept it to himself. He knew that what him and Lauren had going on was sure to make Charmaine feel some type of way. Rico knew that aside from that, what was about to go down today would hurt Charmaine deeply, but it had to be done. He couldn't think about the tears she would cry or all the bad thoughts she would have of him. He just had to man up, block all of that out, and do what he set out to do. Rico had been planning this for months, and it was too late to turn back. He just had to hope that Charmaine wouldn't hold a grudge and that in the end, it would all work out for everyone.

Rico pulled up at the office and got out of Charmaine's car. When he walked inside of the building, he found Lauren packing some things up. "This your last day at this spot?" he inquired.

"Yeah. I see you're right on time. I like a punctual man."

Rico rubbed his hands together and smiled wide. "I'm excited to see what you have for me."

Lauren looked up at him, and her wide smile mirrored his. They were both excited about what was about to go down. "Oh, you're going to love what I have for you. Let me clean the rest of this out, and we can be on our way."

That's what Rico wanted to hear. When Lauren was done, he grabbed a box for her and followed her out to her car. The entire time he walked behind her, all he could think was got damn. Her ass was fat as hell and a great pleasure to look at.

"I CAN'T BELIEVE IT'S YOUR LAST DAY, I'M GOING TO MISS YOU," Charmaine's co-worker, Victoria said as they clocked out and walked together towards the exit.

Charmaine worked in housekeeping at the hospital, and it was never her favorite job but after covid came, shit got real. She literally became afraid every day to go to work because she feared contracting a deadly virus and possibly taking it back home to her kids. Cleaning rooms after people died from the disease was even worse, and so many times she wanted to quit. She had made it though, and now she could finally leave and not feel guilty about it.

Charmaine was instantly agitated when she got out to the

parking lot and didn't see Rico waiting in her car. "I told this nigga to be on time," she mumbled feeling like a fool. She was now that girl. The one that got dropped off at work while a nigga had her car doing God knows what.

Charmaine looked at her watch and saw that it was 5:03. She pulled her cell phone from her purse and tried to call him. When he didn't answer, she grunted and growled in frustration. He was only a few minutes late, but she didn't care. He was supposed to be there at five and not a minute after. This was why you couldn't do people favors, she thought. Charmaine attempted to call him again and once again, he didn't answer. The more time that passed, the angrier she became. Charmaine counted to ten in her head and tried to calm herself down. There had to be a good reason for this. Maybe he had underestimated traffic and was on his way. But why not answer the phone? Maybe because he had Lauren's legs draped over his shoulders while he was digging in her pussy. That thought had Charmaine damn near foaming at the mouth. If Rico had the audacity to cheat on her while he was in possession of her car, she'd fuck him good, and she put that on her kids.

By 5:45 Charmaine's eyes were filled with tears as she called Rico for the third time. Was he hurt? Had he played her? She didn't know, but she couldn't just keep standing there crying. She had to go get her kids, and she wasn't trying to pay a late fee. Even though she had a little money now, being wasteful with it wasn't something that Charmaine was a huge fan of. There was a ten-minute wait for the uber, and she prayed that she would make it to her kids on time. As the minutes ticked by, Charmaine stared at her phone as if her doing so could make it ring. She loved Rico. She really did, but if he didn't have a good excuse for this, she was done with him. It would break her heart if everyone that had told her not to trust him was right. If Rico was just a smoother version of her kid's fathers, that might be the very thing to break her.

Inside the Uber, Charmaine felt as if she was suffocating. It had taken her fairytale one week to end. Only one measly week before trouble entered the relationship. Charmaine felt foolish. She had been through this twice, and she was tired of letting men disappoint her to the point of depression but damn. Why couldn't she win for losing? Why was she so unlucky in love? Charmaine really wanted to know. She arrived at the daycare at 6:29, and she wanted to kill Rico with her bare hands. Having to pay a total of $48 to get from her job to the daycare and then get home. Charmaine was so mad that her face was burning. Inside the house, she washed her hands and began cooking dinner for the kids. She wasn't sure if she should be worried or pissed. Was she stupid to be concerned that he might be hurt? Unless he was dead, he could find a way to communicate with her. Nah, this nigga had simply gassed her up and done her dirty. A tear rolled down her face as she called his phone again. If he wanted to go on about his business then cool, but he could have at least given her damn car back to her. It wasn't even like it was something foreign for him to stunt in.

"Where is your car?" her mother asked when she came into the house and found Charmaine feeding the kids.

She was going to feel like a complete and utter fool once her mother finished telling her how stupid she was. Charmaine wasn't even able to look her mother in the eyes as she mumbled. "I let Rico drive it, and I haven't heard from him since earlier."

Nicole stared at her child. She stared at her without speaking for almost a full minute. Finally, she said, "Well, call the police and report it stolen."

Charmaine shifted her weight from her left leg to her right leg. "I really don't want to do that."

Nicole's tongue clicked against the roof of her mouth. "You know, I didn't want to say I told you so. We've all had to learn but you my dear are determined to learn the extremely hard way. You're grown and if that's the path you want to take then so be it. But you are one damn fool to be sitting up here trying to protect a man that has shown you he clearly doesn't give a damn about you. Tonight, I'm going to get down on these old ass knees and pray that one day very soon, you stop being so damn weak for a man." Nicole turned and walked away after making Charmaine feel even worse.

She felt like a fool. A stupid stupid fool. Her mother had been harsh, but it was no one's fault but her own. Maybe tough love was what she needed. Something had to give and finally click in Charmaine's head that maybe a happily ever after wasn't in the cards for her after all.

Chapter
SEVEN

The next morning, Charmaine was grateful that she didn't have to go to work for many reasons. For one, she had a pounding headache. For two, she still didn't have her car and as much as she didn't want to, she was going to have to call and report it stolen. She knew her mother pitied her when she offered to take the kids to daycare. That was some shit she'd never done before. While Charmaine brushed her teeth, she kept hearing Tookie's voice in her head over and over about Rico being a scammer. A thought came to Charmaine while she was getting dressed, and it felt like someone had punched her in the chest. She grabbed her cell phone with shaky hands and went to the contacts. After touching Lauren's name, she waited to see if the woman would answer. Charmaine needed to know if she had heard from or seen Rico. No answer.

"Why the fuck is no one answering the phone all of a sudden?" Charmaine growled to herself. She hadn't been this pissed off in a long ass time.

What was upsetting her even more was that she'd have to spend more money on an Uber, but she was going by the office. Lauren wouldn't have to answer the phone because Charmaine was going to pop up on her ass. She was so pissed she couldn't even eat breakfast. Charmaine didn't want food, she wanted answers. If she didn't get any from Lauren, then she would just call and report the car stolen. Another thought occurred to her. Why hadn't she thought of it before? The halfway house! If Rico hadn't shown up the night before then he was already in trouble. Her going by there couldn't make it any worse. Besides whatever happened to him, he would have brought the shit on himself. The Uber came, and Charmaine headed to Lauren's office first. She was sure her money hadn't made more than a few hundred dollars if that much, but she was going to tell Lauren to just give her, her shit back. Fuck all this investing and listening to Rico. Charmaine wanted her money in her possession. Forget flipping it.

When Charmaine arrived at Lauren's office, her heart sank into her belly. "No. No. No," she kept repeating over and over to herself. She pulled on the door frantically, but it was locked. In the window was a sign that she'd never seen before. *Daily office rental.* Lauren had been renting that office by the day. It wasn't even a permanent location. They played her. They played the fuck out of her. Charmaine placed one hand on her chest. It felt like she was having a heart attack. Fuck Rico. She wanted her money back. He could get the hell on, and she'd never again in life date. Charmaine was done with men. She would never be in another relationship or get married. She would never have any more children, and that was just fine with her. Charmaine promised God right then, that she'd stop seeking validation from men. She'd stop hoping and praying for a man, and she'd just focus on herself and her kids, if she could just get her money back.

Charmaine got back in the Uber and gave him the address of the halfway house. In the past two days, she'd spent a total of almost $150 on Ubers because a fuck nigga had her car, and she didn't know where he was. Oh no baby. She wasn't going to feel bad at all about calling the police on Rico's ass. She might actually enjoy the shit, and she was going to call the police on Lauren's hoe ass too. Charmaine wanted to scream. She wanted to fight and some mo' shit. Instead of doing any of that, she just remained calm and rode to the next destination. When they arrived at the halfway house, Charmaine didn't see her car out front. Each time she thought she couldn't be disappointed any more than what she already was, she managed to break the previous record. She wasn't that far from her aunt's house, so Charmaine told the Uber he could leave. It was cold outside, and she had about a seven mile trek, but she didn't care. Walking was the only way for her to blow off the steam that was brewing inside of her. Walking would calm her down because by the time she reached her aunt's home, she'd be too tired to cry or want to fight. Charmaine was glad that she had money in the bank to buy another car, and that's what she planned to do anyway, but not like this. She didn't deserve to have her car stolen from her or to be scammed, but maybe she deserved it. All of the red flags were there, but she chose to ignore them because she wanted love so badly.

Charmaine knocked on the door and a few moments later, a dark-skin woman with big eyes answered the door looking confused. She wasn't sure who this woman was, but the men staying at the house weren't allowed visitors. "May I help you?"

"One of the guys that stays here, Rico Nichols. I let him use my car yesterday, and I haven't heard anything from him. I just wanted to know if he was here, so I can ask him where my car is."

"I don't know anything about a car dear, and Nichols didn't come in last night which was a violation of his release. If he does come back here, I'll be calling his parole officer to come pick his ass up."

Charmaine felt so defeated, she couldn't even cry. All she could do was turn and walk away. Two days before Christmas, he pulls this shit. Charmaine began her walk and she was so upset and so numb that the bite from the cold weather wasn't even bothering her. Her legs burned, her feet ached, but she never slowed her stride. In fact, she welcomed the discomfort. It was better than the mental anguish that she was feeling. The heartbreak and betrayal inflicted by Rico was a feeling that was ten times more torturous than the way the walk made her feel. At her aunt's house, Charmaine sat down on the porch to catch her breath. She knew her aunt would have a million questions, and Charmaine dreaded answering any of them. She also wanted to call the police and report her car stolen before she went inside. Before Charmaine could do so, her phone rang. She damn near screamed when she saw that Lauren was calling her. Maybe this bitch wasn't a fraud after all.

"Hi, Charmaine, it's Lauren."

"Yeah, I know who it is. I went by the office, and you weren't there. It seems that it's a daily rental place, and you're not permanently located there."

"I'm not. I don't need an office to do what I do. All I need is a computer, but I don't want to meet with clients in my home or even places like Starbuck's. I rent offices as needed. I hope that won't be a problem for you."

"Not at all because I want my money out. I don't know where Rico is. He took my car, and I haven't heard from him since yesterday. No offense to you, but I don't trust shit affiliated with him right now."

"None taken, but that's actually why I'm calling you. Rico asked me to."

Charmaine's heart slammed into her chest. Rico hadn't gotten in contact with her, but he'd called this bitch?!She knew she had every right to be insecure. Men like Rico always went for women like Lauren. "Rico asked you to call me?!" Charmaine screeched. "Yeah. Y'all got me fucked all the way up."

"I'm not sure what's going on," Lauren spoke slowly, but Rico called me this morning and told me to tell you where you can go get your car from. Whatever the reason, it won't be there until tomorrow. I think it has to be towed." Charmaine wanted to find Rico and rip his balls off. Just that fast, she hated his ass, and she knew it wouldn't be that hard to get over him. She was so mad that she couldn't speak, and Lauren had to wonder if she was still there. "Hello?"

"Give me the address for the car," Charmaine snapped. Maybe Lauren didn't ask to be involved in this, but Charmaine was pissed. She wasn't going to be on any fake ass polite bullshit. Lauren gave her the address to get her car from, and she put it in her phone. "When can I get my money?" she asked after she added the address to her notes.

"Being that tomorrow is a holiday and a weekend we can meet Monday."

Charmaine wanted to curse her out, but she didn't. Instead, she ended the call. When she met with Lauren and got her money, she just might whoop her ass anyway. Something was up with that bitch. Maybe Laurena and Rico had teamed up to play her all along. Yeah, somebody was gon' pay for this shit. Charmaine was tired of going out like a weak bitch behind a nigga.

THE NEXT MORNING CHARMAINE RODE IN THE UBER AND HEADED for the address to get her car. It was Christmas Eve, and she had helped her mother start prepping the food for Christmas dinner. She promised the kids they'd bake cookies when she got back. Charmaine was going to enjoy her holiday, but Rico was dead to her. Monday, she would go find an apartment for her and the kids, get a new car, wait to start school, and never look back. She wasn't going to be one of those frumpy ass old maids. She was going to boss up and be successful and fine. Men would for sure try her, and she'd take great pleasure in turning them all down. A man would never get the chance to play her or make her look stupid again, and Charmaine put that on everything. When the Uber pulled into a nice neighborhood, her stomach began to churn. Something was telling her that her car was at a bitch's house, and she would bet money that bitch was named Lauren. This neighborhood was nice as hell. Who did Rico know that lived here? Why did her car have to be towed here? The Uber pulled up in the driveway of a beautiful brick home. Her car wasn't in the driveway, and she knew he must have the wrong address. There were two cars in the driveway. A red beamer and a black Range Rover. The Range had a red bow on it, and Charmaine was baffled. This had to be a mistake. She was tired of the cat and mouse games. She just wanted her car and her money, so she could be done with this shit. Just as she opened her mouth to tell the Uber driver that this must be the wrong place, the door to the house opened, and Lauren stepped out on the porch with a smile. Charmaine knew it!

She would feel like such a bad mother if she spent Christmas in jail, but she was gon' beat this hoe's ass. Charmaine damn near broke a nail getting out of the car. She rushed up towards the porch ready to slap the smile off Lauren's smug face. "Surprise!"

Charmaine stopped dead in her tracks. Her eyes darted

around before her gaze landed back on Lauren's face. "What the fuck you mean surprise?"

"Merry Christmas from Rico. This is your new home, and that's your new truck." Lauran spoke while pointing to the Range Rover.

"But how? With what? Charmaine managed to utter, while still unsure what was going on.

Well I can tell you it wasn't with your invested money, if that's what you are asking. Rico from my understanding has been investing with Josh for sometime now and has seen a very nice profit. Josh is my mentor and showed me everything I know about crypto and investing. So I'm sure Rico has seen some great returns on his money. When he met you, he wanted to help you. He had to make sure you were worth it first. That's why he asked you to invest the money. To see if you would, simply because he asked you to. It was a big gamble for the both of you to take, but it told him a lot about you. He sees how hard you work and how your kid's fathers don't help you. He just wanted to show you how much he loved you and that all men are not the same."

Charmaine erupted into tears. That's why he didn't want her to get a place. Charmaine felt like she was dreaming. Him running off with her money would have made more sense. What was happening now, she couldn't fathom. Her life had never been that good. No one had ever had her back that much, and it was very much surreal to her. All she could do was cry. Charmaine felt a hand rubbing her back, and Lauren's expensive perfume infiltrated her nostrils. Charmaine's head snapped up. "Where is Rico?"

"He turned himself back into the the prison. He wasn't feeling being on papers. He wasn't feeling being in the halfway house or having to deal with a PO. I think he said he has like six months and he'll be free and clear. Come in let me show you the house. I also do a little interior designing." Lauren winked at Charmaine. "I'm something like a hustler."

It did Charmaine no good to wipe her tears with the back of her hand because every time she did, more fell. The water works wouldn't stop. She really felt as if she was floating on air. Never in a million years had she expected this! It was absolutely the best Christmas that she ever had in her entire life. Charmaine was bawling like a baby. The relief that came from her knowing that Rico hadn't done her dirty had her dizzy. She was worthy of love. Someone had come along and shown her that all men weren't the same. Inside the house, Charmaine gasped. Everything that she described to him over the phone on those long prison conversations had come to fruition. He had remembered every minor detail and relayed it to Lauren. Charmaine could understand him not wanting to stay in the halfway house, and he had told her how his PO was trying to violate him for any reason. But she wanted nothing more in that moment than to have Rico by her side. She wanted to take him into one of the rooms and suck his dick and to give him some pussy. He deserved it! He had gone all out and spared no expense on the furniture and décor. The living room looked like something from a magazine. Lauren led her into the bathroom next, and Charmaine smiled at the yellow décor. It was warm and inviting. The kitchen melted her heart. The stainless steel appliances and red décor was everything. By the time they got to the kids' rooms, she was crying again. Charmaine had to lean up against the wall to keep from collapsing onto the floor. She was so overwhelmed from the emotion that her knees buckled.

She for sure was going to buy Rico an eighteen wheeler, put him through trucking school, or do whatever she needed to do to prove that she was in fact down for him. Lauren said he wasn't broke, but neither was she. Charmaine had no problem spoiling and investing in a man that had done the same for her.

She already had plans to fill his side of the closet with clothes and shoes for when he came home. Charmaine knew her kids were going to love the house, and she couldn't wait to see the look on her mother's face when she saw it!

"I can move in right away?" Charmaine asked Lauren once the tour ended.

"You sure can. You feel how warm and toasty it is in here? Rico made sure all the utilities were on before he turned himself in. He refused to go back in until the house was ready for you and the kids."

Her phone rang, and she saw that she had a call showing No Caller ID, this had to be Rico calling from the prison. Charmaine had never answered a call so fast in her life. She held her breath while she waited for them to be connected. "Baby, I love you!" She screamed into the phone, and Rico laughed.

"I take it you've seen the house."

"I'm here now. No one has ever done anything even halfway this special for me. You will never know how much I appreciate you, and I will spend the rest of my life letting you know that I have your back always and forever. Baby, I love you so much. I'm sad you went back in, but I can patiently wait for you to come home."

"I told you from day one you had to trust me, right? You took a hell of a chance on me. Through people talking shit and telling you not to trust me, you stood ten toes down for a nigga. I appreciated that, and I wasn't about to give anybody a reason to clown you. I can only imagine how you felt yesterday when I didn't show up with your car. I hated to put you through that, but I wanted this to be a serious ass surprise."

"If I could have gotten my hands on you yesterday, it would have been all bad," she laughed. "I'm coming to see you next week and every week after that. I won't miss a visit for the next six months."

"I'm going to hold you to that."

"I don't know what I did to deserve you."

"You didn't give up. Not even after two fuck boys gave you every reason not to believe in love anymore. They gave you every reason to swear off love and to not give anyone else a chance, but you took a major one with me. An inmate. You made the last year of my sentence something special. It's only right that I show you how real niggas get down and when I come home, it's only up from there. You've been Superwoman long enough. You can rest now, ma."

Charmaine laughed through her tears. "I'm so tired of crying."

"You don't have to do that shit no more. Merry Christmas baby."

The automated system alerted them that they had sixty seconds left, and Charmaine wasn't even mad. One thing she had learned through all of this was patience, and she had an entire lifetime to go with Rico.

"You never called." Candice smirked as she entered Rico's pod. He was laid back on his bunk with his arms behind his head.

He really hated prison. Some thought he was a damn fool for going back in but as long as he was on papers, he wasn't really free. He had every intention of going home and doing the right thing. But his Parole officer had made it clear that he wasn't interested in hearing about Rico's idea of trucking driving school. Rather he wanted him to get a job Immediately. Even though Rico showed him that he had the funds to secure himself financially, his PO didn't care. Rico knew that this wasn't going to work for him and the big plans he had for himself and Charmaine. So going back and finishing his time was definitely the best option. He didn't want to be on papers period. As long as he'd gotten Charmaine set up on the outside, that's all he really cared about. She proved to him that she was solid, and he had now proved the same to her. Rico had no doubt in his mind that he would come home to a great woman and that he'd get to live the family life with no fear of ever going back to prison.

"Yeah, I didn't really get a chance to." Rico responded now clicking back to Candice's question.

Candice shook her head. "I see you came back though. I thought I told you not to do that. Seems you did the opposite of everything that I wanted you to do."

"I didn't come back because I fucked up. I came back by choice. But once I walk up out of those gates next time, best believe I'm never coming back."

"So, why didn't you call? Is it because of the female that comes to visit you?"

"Yeah it was. I just wanted to get her set up nice and spend some time with her. The short time that I was out there, my main objective was to make sure she had a great Christmas. I wasn't really concerned with much else."

Candice's eyebrows shot up. That's not what she expected to hear, but she could respect it. Maybe Rico was a good one after all, and they were rare as hell. "Sounds like she's a lucky woman."

"Nah I'm the lucky one" He responded with a smile, just thinking about Charmaine.

Candice saw men play women every day at the prison. It was nothing for an inmate to have two or three different women all coming to visit him on different weeks, and he would be in the visitation room hugging and kissing on all of them while selling them the same dreams. She saw inmates getting cards and letters from numerous women, and every man damn near promised marriage when they came home. Some of the ones with super long bids even talked their woman into marrying them while they were in prison. She would have loved to let Rico sample the kitty while he was out in the free world, but she had to respect him being true to Charmaine. Candice nodded her head at Rico and left his pod.

Once he was alone, Rico sat up and grabbed his CDL truck driving study book. He was determined not to waste this time in prison. He was going to come home on his A game in every way.

Chapter EIGHT

Rico stared across the table at his girlfriend, Charmaine. The scent of her perfume filled his nostrils, and all he could think about was how good her pussy lips had felt wrapped around his dick. The short amount of time he spent with her, after getting out of prison, played heavily on his mind day in and day out. Sometimes, he couldn't believe that he voluntarily came back to this hell hole just so he wouldn't be on parole once he was released. Charmaine had always been an attractive woman, but now that she was financially straight, she had really upped her game and was a stunner for real. Her nails were long, dramatic, and blinged out. Her long weave had a part in the middle and was draped over her shoulders in loose curls. It looked like she had just left the salon; not a strand of hair was out of place. Her brows were freshly waxed, lashes done, and she had on jeans that hugged her curvaceous frame, a cream turtleneck cashmere sweater, and cream thigh-high boots. As soon as she stood up to give him a hug, Rico's dick got hard. With the iced-out watch on her wrist, the diamonds in her ears, Charmaine looked like that chick and Rico was happy for her and himself. She deserved all the pampering and security that she now experienced and a smile came over his face knowing he was partially responsible. They believed in each other and now were enjoying the fruits of their love and faith.

"Got damn, you looking good, ma. You got me feeling like I played the fuck out of myself by coming back in this bitch," he stated, almost regretfully. Only a week had passed since he came back to prison, and he had brought in the New Year in a hard, cold cell instead of at home with his girl.

"I hate that you felt like you had to come back in here, baby, but I understand why you did it. I pray that these six months go by super fast." Charmaine detested that he'd made the sole decision to finish his sentence in prison, but at this point, there was nothing she could do about it. In Rico's mind, he knew that consulting her wouldn't have been smart because what woman would want her man locked back up. He now understood not allowing her to have a say in the matter was the wrong decision.

Rico ran one hand over his waves. "Time has never gone by fast in this muhfucka, but I just gotta hold my head and do my bid. It's good seeing you though. You look good as fuck." His eyes roamed over her breasts.

Charmaine smiled bashfully and dropped her head. All of the compliments from Rico made her feel extremely good. There were too many times she came to see him feeling dusty. Too many times her nails needed a fill, or she had to wear her hair slicked up in a bun because she didn't have money to get it done. With all the time she'd spent struggling, Charmaine was enjoying all the extra money she had from the sale of her grandmother's house. What made it even better was since Rico had gone behind her back and got her a house and a car. She hadn't had to use any of her own money. He also had set up for the monthly bills to be paid by his accountant, Lauren. For the first time ever, Charmaine had plenty of money and no bills, but she was being smart. She had enrolled in school, and her first day was the following morning.

"Thank you, baby. You look good yourself. I can't wait for you to bench press me like you do those weights," she flirted, and he chuckled.

"Trust me, ma. You're light work. I can lift that ass with no problem." He winked.

Charmaine gazed into his eyes. "On a serious note, baby. I hate the fact that after you made Christmas so special for me, you had to spend it alone. Did at least your family come to visit you?" It had dawned on Charmaine a few times when she thought Rico stole her money, that she didn't know a lot about his family. She didn't know how to get in contact with his mom, dad, siblings, or anyone.

"Nah, I don't really get visits like that." Rico shrugged one shoulder passively.

"Your mom, your siblings, nobody comes?" she probed.

Family was a touchy subject for Rico, but he understood that he was no longer some guy that simply talked to Charmaine on the phone and got to visit with her a few times a month. He had dropped a lot of money on a house and a car for her—a house that he would be living in with her and her kids once he came home, so they had to talk about the uncomfortable stuff.

"My grandmother raised me. My mom wasn't on drugs or anything, but she was young and uninterested in being a mother. I was born in Atlanta. My mom lived there with her father. She got pregnant with me at seventeen, and she came here to live with her mom. When I was six months old, she decided she wanted to go back to the A, and she asked my grandmother to keep me while she got a job and got on her feet. My grandmother didn't mind because she didn't fully trust my mom anyway when it came to parenting. It ended up taking her ten years to get on her feet and even when she sent for me, it was only for the summer. My first night there, she left me home by myself, so she could go clubbing. I called my grandma because I got hungry, and a woman that is deathly afraid of planes, flew to get me, cursed my mom the hell out, and never let me go with her again."

"Damn," Charmaine mumbled.

"I think my mom was mad at me for telling because she didn't call to check up on me or talk to me for almost a year after that. Once she finally came around again, my attitude was really indifferent towards her. Even to this day, I'll talk to her, but I don't fuck with her like that. My grandmother raised me, and that's who I look at as my mother, but she doesn't want anything to do with me right now."

Charmaine's interest piqued. "Why not?"

Rico licked his lips. He hated telling this story. He hated how he had disappointed his grandmother after all she had ever done for him. "The church that she goes to, she's been a member there for years. She ended up getting a position in the office, and she had access to some important information from some of the members. Names of course, addresses, and for some of them, their financial information. When I got knocked for credit card fraud and all that, the church found out that it was me that had cards and bank accounts and shit in some of the members' names, which caused them to side eye my grandma. She was embarrassed as hell, and she hasn't spoken to me since."

"Damn," Charmaine repeated again. "I'm sorry to hear that."

"I can't really be mad at her. I violated. It was some selfish shit to do, and I put her name and reputation on the line for some fast money. The first few months of my bid, I was mad as fuck at her and wrote her a letter sayin' how she was a hypocrite for not forgiving me because that's what the church teaches. I was young, angry, and immature at that time and was blaming everyone but myself. When I finally wised up and realize how I had put her in a fucked-up situation and she was justified in being angry and not trusting my ass anymore, it was too late, she had totally cut me off. Although I'm sorry for what I did, and I would never violate like that again, how is she supposed to know that?"

Rico's eyes began to water. He truly looked sorry, and Charmaine really felt bad for him. She could tell from the pain his face held that he was bothered by his strained relationship with his grandmother, and he took full accountability. "Well, babe, you are definitely not that person, and I think she'd love the man you've become today. You don't think she'll come around?" Charmaine asked hopefully.

"I really don't know, baby. And I have to accept that. I know I'm not one of God's favorite people, but I've prayed and asked Him plenty to touch her heart on my behalf. I even wrote the church a check when I first started getting my investment payments for the losses I caused. That's all I can do."

Charmaine squeezed his hand and gave Rico a comforting smile. "She'll come around. I know she will. People change, and you have done just that. I'm a witness. Only a person with a heart of gold would do what you did for me and my kids."

Charmaine and Rico switched topics, and time flew by. Before they both knew it, they were hugging goodbye. As Rico inhaled Charmaine's perfume, he wished that he was out in the world with her. Shit, with the way she had come into her own, without a doubt niggas were trying to crack on her. Rico never wanted to be a fool for anybody. Charmaine was a good girl, but there was only so much temptation one could take. Before, Charmaine was working like a dog, juggling two jobs, and visiting him in her free time. She was always tired and always stressed. Now, she didn't have to work, so she would only be going to school for a few hours a day, and she had plenty of money at her disposal. Rico would be lying if he said he wasn't slightly worried about her being out there alone for the next few months.

Meanwhile, as Charmaine switched out to her new Range Rover courtesy of Rico, another man was the last thing on her mind. She wanted her man home with her. Charmaine wanted to spend each night riding that long, thick dick. Then, she wanted to fall asleep in his muscular arms, and she didn't want to have to wait half of a year for it. Rico had stepped up to the plate in a major way and made her dreams come true. Now, she was going to see if it was possible for her to do the same for him.

Chapter NINE

Charmaine closed her eyes and counted to ten in her head. She tried very hard to be respectful of her mother, but Nicole was really pushing it.

"You don't have to act funny, Charmaine. I know you out there with the white people living life the lifestyle of the rich and the famous, but I don't want to drive the car if you don't want me to have it."

"Momma, if I didn't want you to have the car, I wouldn't have told you that you could get it." Charmaine tried to keep her tone respectful. "I also told you that the battery was dead. I don't know how to jump a car, but it seems to me if you were that pressed, you'd send someone out here to jump it, but that's on me too, right?" Charmaine was losing her cool. She knew firsthand how it felt to be down and out, so selfish was something she wasn't. And she certainly wasn't acting funny, but since she came up, people were coming out of the woodworks acting entitled like she owed them something, and Charmaine didn't like that shit one bit.

"Oh, I know you done lost your mind talking to me like that. My how soon we forget. It was just a few weeks ago that you were living in my house, off of me."

"I was working two jobs. Living with you and living off you are two different things. And Momma, I have told you over and over how thankful I was and am for what you did for me. I gotta go though. It'll be my pleasure to get this car running and towed to you. After that, it's on you, and I think that's fair."

Charmaine ended the call before her mother could respond. Her patience was running very thin. A cousin that she hadn't spoken to in years, saw her in her Range and had the nerve to DM her on Instagram two days later asking to borrow five hundred dollars. Charmaine didn't understand the nerve of people. When she was doing bad, she literally only had about two people she could call, and that was it. Now, all of a sudden, everyone had their hands out. Charmaine wasn't selfish, but she wasn't a fool either. She knew she was by no means rich. Although she now had some savings and the opportunity to be financially stable, she wasn't in any position to take care of others.

"Micah, stop taking your sister's cookies," Charmaine scolded her son as she looked up numbers for the nearest tow shop.

She called and arranged to get the car towed, then she gave the kids a bath and read them a story. It wasn't even dark outside yet, but she had homework to do, and she wanted them to wind down for the night. After she read them a story, she put a movie on for them, and grabbed her laptop and her books. Now that she didn't have to be worried with work, she could really focus, and Charmaine's aim was to be a straight A student. Life was definitely so much easier since she wasn't robbing Peter to pay Paul or worrying about where her next dollar was coming from. Every time she got in her car or looked around her house, she just wanted to tongue Rico down then suck his dick. After dealing with and having kids by two dead-beat ass losers, Rico had shown her what a real man was, and she would love him forever for that shit. There was no one that could make her turn her back on him. So, even though she wasn't thrilled to have to wait another six months for him to come home, she was going to hold him down no questions asked.

Charmaine heard a loud noise, and when she looked out of the living room window, she saw that the tow truck had arrived. Charmaine put her book on the couch and went to open the door. She stepped outside and when the dude hopped out of the truck, she immediately recognized Sammy's cousin, Jonah, and she held in a groan. Sammy was Micah's dad. A person that put the B in bum. She hadn't seen Sammy in about five months, and he hadn't even gotten his son anything for Christmas. She could tell from the gleam in Jonah's little beady eyes that he was impressed.

"What up, Charmaine? Damn, you living out here now?" He looked around the neighborhood in awe.

"Yeap," she replied dryly, "with my nigga," Charmaine added, wanting to make sure he knew that, just in case he or one of his grimy ass friends got the idea to try and run up in there. Now she wished she had chosen a different company, but it was too late.

"Okay, I see you. My lil' cousin in the house?"

Charmaine frowned up her face in disgust. Sammy's entire family acted as if Micha didn't exist. Now, Jonah was calling him lil' cousin. *Fuck outta here,* she thought to herself. "Can we speed this up? I have something to do." Charmaine was extra glad she had a security system and a gun. She didn't trust Jonah's rat looking ass one bit.

Her house was big, and she would have been afraid to stay

in it alone if it wasn't for the security system. As soon as the alarm went off to alert her that someone was trying to come in her shit, she was going to shoot first and ask questions last.

"You don't even have to be like that. I don't have anything to do with what you and Sammy have going on. Micah is still my family though."

Charmaine ignored him. Sammy and anyone related to him literally made her blood boil. It was nobody's financial responsibility to take care of Micha except her and Sammy. She didn't fault anyone in his family for not giving her money, but they didn't even pick up the phone and ask how her son was doing. Even her evil ass mother would call to make sure the kids were good if too many days passed without her seeing Charmaine and the kids. There were no excuses for being deadbeat all the way around, and they could all kiss Charmaine's ass. She stood in the driveway, lips sealed, acting as if Jonah wasn't even there until he'd assessed what was wrong with the car.

"You need a new battery. I can sell you one and put it in before I tow the car."

Charmaine started to tell him to just tow the shit and let her ungrateful ass mother pay for a battery, but she was going to be the bigger person. "How much?" she asked in a gruff voice.

"The battery and labor charge will be $150 even. Then the towing will be $0.36 a mile."

"Cool."

It was cold out, so Charmaine left him in the driveway and watched him from the door as he worked. When he was done, she took the cash out to him, signed the paper attached to the clipboard he handed her, and switched her ass back in the house like her shit didn't stink. She knew his mouthy ass would run straight to Sammy and let him know that she was living in a nice house and pushing a Range. Sammy and her other baby daddy, Bruno, had been dead to her. She wouldn't piss on them if they were on fire, but it felt good to know that the gossip

Jonah would carry back wouldn't be bad. He couldn't say he saw her looking raggedy and doing bad, which made her smile.

WHEN JONAH PULLED UP AT HIS AUNT MONA'S HOUSE AND SAW Sammy sitting on the porch smoking a cigarette, he hopped out of his truck ready to gossip like the bitch that he was. "Yoooo brah, guess who the fuck I saw today?"

Sammy could tell by the animated tone of Jonah's voice that whatever he was about to say was good. "Nigga, who?" He wasn't about to play guessing games.

"Your baby moms, and that muhfucka done came all the way up, my nigga." Sammy's ears perked up. Jonah rubbed his hands together and leaned up against the house. "Shorty live in a nice ass crib, and she pushing a Range, my nigga. She had her old whip towed to her mom's house. I'm asking her does she live there, and she like yeah, she live there with her nigga. Dude must have major money. Those houses out that way start at like $600,000. And that Range," he kissed his teeth in an animated fashion, "it's one of the new joints. Peanut butter leather seats. That bitch is pretty." He shook his head, and Sammy's interest was all the way piqued.

"Who her nigga?" he asked as he pulled from the cigarette.

"I have no clue, but she can't have a crib like that by herself. Just last year, she was pushing that lil' rusty, beat up ass Honda Civic. Now, she in a new crib, and she has a Range. I'm asking her about Micha, and shorty was acting real stank too."

"Word?" The wheels in Sammy's head were turning.

When Sammy and Charmaine met, he was twenty. Sammy was a low-level corner hustler, who could only afford his cell phone bill, weed to smoke every day, cigarettes, and clothes and shoes. He lived with his mother, and drove a fifteen-year-old car. At the time, Charmaine was young too. She didn't care that

Sammy didn't have much. She had a job that supplied her needs; he would take her on cheap dates and get her hair and nails done, and she was fine with that. Until she got pregnant. Charmaine wanted her own place, and she applied for low income housing. Sammy was happy because he could finally move out of his mother's house without the worry of a lot of expenses. Charmaine applied for food stamps, and he was living the life. He hustled hard to get her some cheap furniture, but soon, the bare minimum that he was providing wasn't enough to keep her satisfied.

Charmaine got up every day and went to work big belly and all, while he hung in the hood, selling drugs, gambling, and smoking weed. When it was time to start buying things for the baby, that's where most of her paychecks would go. The first time she asked Sammy to pay her full $236 rent, he damn near had a fit, and she realized that she was with a bum ass nigga. The final straw came when it was time to get the baby's bassinet. It was $160, and they were supposed to go half. Sammy came home and told her that he lost all his money on the card table, and she put him out.

Charmaine was disgusted, and she refused to keep letting a man live off of her. As soon as she found out she was going to be somebody's mother, her motherly instincts activated. She started planning and acting like a parent. Too bad the same couldn't be said for her child's father. From that day forward, Sammy was salty. He wasn't a man at all, and Charmaine required too much of him. There wasn't an ambitious bone in his body. He had watched his mother struggle his entire life, and that was the norm for him. He didn't care about having nice, expensive furniture. He didn't care about having a savings account or burial insurance. He just wanted to dress in the latest fashions and smoke the finest weed. That's it. Those were his goals. When he had to go back to his mom's house, he became bitter, and refused to help Charmaine with Micha. In the last year or so, he'd come around just a tad. There were times he wanted to get his son, but Charmaine wouldn't let him go. Rather than taking accountability, Sammy put all the blame on her and pegged her to be a trifling baby mama. But upon hearing that her and her kids were living with some nigga and were doing so well, a surge of jealousy shot through Sammy that surprised even him.

"What's that address?"

Chapter
TEN

Charmaine hadn't been to church in a long time, but she figured Wednesday night prayer service would be a good time to start. She had to admit that the pastor's short sermon hit home for her. The message was about perseverance. No matter how many times she cried in the past and wanted to give up, she held on and did what she had to for herself and kids. In the end, it had paid off, and she could only thank God for that. When the service was over, she remembered why she had come in the first place, and Charmaine was sweating bullets, but she reasoned with herself that Rico's grandmother looked too sweet to curse her out in church. Charmaine didn't want to keep bringing up a subject that was obviously very hard for Rico, so she asked him just enough questions so she could do her own research. She was able to find out what church Ms. Mary went to, after, she found an old picture and tag of her on Rico's Facebook page. Although the picture was six years old, she still pretty much looked the same. Charmaine took a deep breath and walked up to the elderly woman.

"Ms. Nichols?"

Rico's grandmother looked up at the strange young lady, wondering how she knew her name. "Yes, dear. I'm Ms. Nichols."

"Hi. You don't know me, and please don't get mad, but I'm your grandson, Rico's girlfriend." Charmaine noticed the woman's body stiffen, but she kept talking. "I really don't want to overstep my boundaries, but Rico really is a changed man. He's very sorry for what he did and," Charmaine paused and took a deep breath before she continued, "it would mean the world to him and me, if you would at least talk to him. He misses you so much."

Mary saw that the young woman was scared to death, and that's the only reason she didn't read her the fifth in a Christian way. Her voice remained polite and respectful when she spoke, but the seriousness in her tone was undeniable. "Baby, I raised that boy like he was my own. Gave him everything I had and things that I didn't. I would have rather he stole from me than to do what he did. So many innocent people were affected by his foolishness, and what's worse is, he did it at a place that I worshiped and worked at for more than twenty years. He had people looking at me like I was a thief and the scum of the earth, and I've never stolen anything a day in my life. I pray to God that he has changed because hell is hot, and I'd hate for his soul to be damned there for all of eternity. But I don't have anything to say to my grandson. You have a blessed day, sweetheart. And watch that boy around your purse," she added before walking off.

Charmaine felt defeated. It would have been wonderful if Ms. Mary was open to reconciling with Rico, but Charmaine saw where she was coming from. She'd be heartbroken if one of her kids did that to her, but she also couldn't fathom going years without talking to either of her children. Micha and Morgan were her entire world. Charmaine turned and walked out of the church. All she could do was hope that Rico's grandmother would come around soon. When she thought Rico had stolen her money, her heart was broken. A few people told her she was a fool for trusting him, but Charmaine was glad she went with her gut. Rico might have had a shady past, but he was a good man. Maybe one day, his grandmother would be able to see that.

Charmaine's kids were at her cousin, Nesha's house playing with Nesha's kids. Her cousin had cooked, so Charmaine was going to eat with her. On the way out of the church, she had passed someone and got a whiff of what smelled like moth balls, and Charmaine gagged. Her stomach churned, and she thought she was going to have to run in the restroom and throw up. *What in the hell is wrong with me?* she thought then looked up at the sky. Even if she hadn't said it out loud, she'd thought of a curse word on church grounds. Charmaine looked up as if she expected to see a bolt of lightning. As she walked to her truck with her heels clacking on the pavement, her heart started to race to the rhythm of her steps. The first two times she was pregnant, her smell was extremely sensitive. It was as if she could smell things a mile away, and certain smells like raw meat made her gag. Charmaine sat in her car thinking of all the sex that her and Rico had while he was home for that short period of time. Could she really be pregnant by him?

Just as Charmaine was about to start up her SUV, someone knocked on her window. She looked up and was surprised to see Ms. Mary standing there, motioning for her to roll down the window. Hitting the down button immediately, She prayed that Rico's grandmother had changed her mind.

"Hey, baby we got to talking about Rico, and my Christian spirit left me. I forgot to ask if you currently have a church home?" Charmaine's pause answered the question in Ms. Mary's mind. "I figured you didn't, which is why the Holy Spirit led me back over here. Will you be my guest this Sunday?" Charmaine was definitely caught off guard and all she could do was say yes.

Under any other circumstances, Charmaine would've been terrified at the mere thought of being pregnant. But nothing or anyone could convince her that she'd go through what her other two baby daddies put her through with Rico. Charmaine started her truck anxiously. Before she stopped by Nesha's house, she was surely going to pick up a pregnancy test.

"You gotta hold Mommy's hand, Micha, there's a lot of people walking, baby." Charmaine held onto both of her kids' hands tight as they navigated the crowd that filed out of the church. Again, the word had touched Charmaine's heart, making her tear up as the preacher spoke. She hoped that Ms. Mary felt more open to talk to her today about forgiving Rico. Ms. Mary had saved her and the kids a seat on the front row.

"Wasn't that a beautiful sermon, Ms. Mary," Charmaine spoke as they walked through the church parking lot. Ms. Mary turned around and gave Charmaine a warm smile. "Yes it was baby, and I know what you're getting at." The sermon was about the prodigal son and although Charmaine wasn't an expert, she knew that sermon had to hit home with Rico's grandmother.

"Oh no I didn't mean anything by it." Charmaine chuckled nervously.

Ms. Mary was tough, which she could tell from their interaction. But she saw how much she loved kids by her interaction with her two.

"Hi, babies, aren't y'all just beautiful," she spoke to the children. They both waved back and tried hiding behind Charmaine's legs.

"Yes, these are my two little ones, Micha and Morgan. And we were wondering if we could treat you to lunch.

"Sure, long as handsome here is paying." She nodded towards Micha, and Charmaine laughed.

"I'm sure we can arrange that." The group ended up at a soul food restaurant not too far from the church. "Thank you for accepting the invite."

"Sure. I already know why I'm here."

"That obvious, huh?" Charmaine pulled a piece of her hair behind her ear and handed the kids each a kids menu and crayons to color while she talked.

"Yeah. And I'll admit that I think it's nice of you to want to mend the relationship between my grandson and I, but to be honest with you, sugar, only God can say when it's time."

"I know and I swear I'm not trying to rush it, I just know the pain I saw in Rico's eyes when he talked about you. I can't lie and say that I don't hurt for him." Charmaine wasn't speaking from a place of pity and hoped that Ms. Mary understood that.

Ms. Mary reached across the table and grabbed hold of Charmaine's hand. "Whatever is meant to come out of mine and my grandson's relationship, God will surely handle it. I'm glad that Rico is feeling the strain as he should. When the time is right, it'll happen. Now, tell me about you because anyone willing to run up on me without an invite must be in some kind of love with my grandson." Charmaine chuckled and went on to tell Ms. Mary bits and pieces about herself. They spent the rest of the afternoon laughing and talking about Rico as a child. Ms. Mary had even imparted some words of wisdom on Charmaine. Although she didn't get Rico's grandmother to agree to see him or even take his call, she did feel good about getting to know her.

✳

Rico sat on his bunk scrolling discreetly through his phone. He was looking at all of the naked pictures Charmaine had sent him the night before. Being that he only had six more months to do, Rico really tried hard to walk a straight path. If he got caught with any contraband, they could add more time to his bid easily. He tried to go without a phone though, but he just had to have one. Money talked, and Rico was glad that when he was making fast money, he wasn't blowing it all. His friend turned him onto Lauren, and she was the truth. His money had been making money for him for the past few years, and he had more than tripled his initial investment. When he was finally released for good, he was going to start a business and live the life of a square nigga. Rico had done his share of dirt, and he was ready to put all of that behind him. Looking at Charmaine's pictures had his dick hard and his mouth watering. He had chosen a winner for real, and he couldn't wait to finally be able to be with her without having to worry about home visits from a probation officer, drug tests, or anything else they could come up with to keep tabs on his ass.

Rico was still staring at his phone but soon, he zoned out. He no longer saw Charmaine's naked body. Rather, he found himself wondering if it was worth it. Fast money used to be his drug of choice. He was addicted to that shit and would spend the money as quickly as he would make it. Until something told him to be smart and invest it. Everything Rico now had come from the currency he invested, but the money he'd invested came from doing the one person he loved more than life itself wrong, and he had to ask if it was worth it. Rico told himself everything from no one will ever find out, to he wasn't hurting his grandmother directly, and that had all been a lie. Just some bullshit he convinced himself to believe so he wouldn't feel guilty about what he was doing. Not being able to pick up the phone and call his grandma, hurt, but he was the one at fault and had done it to himself. Rico let out a sigh and pushed the feelings of guilt out of his mind. His eyes focused back on Charmaine, and he needed to hear her voice immediately. Rico couldn't be on the phone long, and he wanted to make sure that it was a good time to call, so he texted her first.

His eyes shot over to the door every few seconds. Most of the correctional officers were cool, but he never knew which one might try to flex just to fuck with him because they knew he didn't have much time left. After about five minutes and no text back, Rico started getting antsy. He decided to just pick up the phone and call her. The phone rang all of three times before a voice answered that had Rico frowning up his face and foaming at the mouth. "Who the fuck is this!" he barked, forgetting all about the fact that he was supposed to be sneaking.

"Nigga, who the fuck is this? This is Sammy. Charmaine's baby daddy."

Rico's whole body felt sick and it was a good thing he wasn't standing because his legs felt weak. Hearing another nigga answering Charmaine's phone felt like he had been shot. He wasn't about to argue with this hoe ass nigga over the phone. He was so angry that he threw the device across the room ,causing it to shatter into pieces.

"Snake ass, hoe ass, bitch!" were the only words he could scream out. Rico grabbed the sheet and balled it up as tight as he could before placing it over his face. The tears were already welling up in his eyes, and he wanted to scream out again in sorrow. He remembered where he was and showing hurt and weakness wasn't allowed here unless you wanted to be a victim. So, he cried quietly the best he could under the coverings of the blanket, until falling off to sleep from pure fatigue.

Chapter ELEVEN

"Another one?" Charmaine looked back and forth between her two kids. "You want me to read another story? I've already read you guys two stories," she asked jokingly

"Just one more pleaseeee, Mommy."

"Okay. Go upstairs and get me one more book to read. After that, Mommy has to do homework." The kids took off running just as the doorbell rang, making Charmaine raise her eyebrows as she stood up.

No one had been to her new home except Nesha and Charmaine's mother. She groaned to herself, hoping that it wasn't Nicole because she didn't have the energy for her mother today. Everyone thought Charmaine was acting brand new because she was no longer struggling, and that wasn't the case. She just didn't have the patience for entitled ass people. Her mother included. When Charmaine looked and saw who was at the door, her heart began to pound irately. To say she was pissed would've been an understatement. She knew exactly how he had gotten her address, and Charmaine snatched the door open furiously. She felt like a rabid dog and wouldn't be surprised if she started foaming at the mouth.

"Get the fuck off my porch, and tell your bitch ass cousin, I'm getting him fired for giving out my address!" Charmaine was so angry, she could have spit nails. He had some nerve showing up at her house unannounced. She didn't care at all about the bags in his hands that she was sure contained some lame ass gifts for Micha. Not after she'd bought him everything he needed and a good majority of everything that he wanted.

"Cousin? I don't know what you're talking about," Sammy played dumb. "I just wanted to come see my son and to give him some gifts. That's all. How you got another nigga in here playing house with my son, and I can't even see him?" Sammy tried to peek inside the house to see just how his baby mama was living. He could tell from the outside of the house alone that her dude had some major paper, and he didn't like that shit at all. Sammy didn't have any feelings for Charmaine, but he still didn't want to see her happy with the next man.

Charmaine narrowed her eyes at the poor excuse of a father standing at her door. "Take those gifts and shove them up your ass, and I mean that from the bottom of my heart. In fact, the only gift that you can give me is the one of signing over your rights to my son. Your broke ass can't even pay me fifty dollars a month in child support. You're a fucking joke." She looked him up and down, and it pissed Sammy off even if what she was saying was true. "Let's just cut all ties with each other, and the child support will be dropped."

"You living like this, what do you need my money for? It's always about money with you bitches. If I'm not up right now, I can't see my own kid? How that shit work?"

"Ha!" Charmaine laughed sarcastically in his face. "If you're not up right now? Nigga ,you've never been up in your entire pathetic ass life. You really are a joke. And I just said if you sign over your rights, the child support will be dropped." Charmaine cut her rant short, and her eyes widened when she heard her kids' voices at the top of the stairs.

She turned around and dashed towards the steps. She wanted to keep Micha upstairs because if he saw Sammy, he would want to spend time with him, and that loser wasn't stepping foot in Charmaine's home. That's where she drew the line. Any other time, she might've been the bigger person and let Sammy see Micha only because it would make her son happy but not today. Charmaine was livid that he even had the balls to show up at her house, and she really was going to call Jonah's job and report him. She prayed to God he got fired since he wanted to be giving out her address. This was just another reason she wanted Rico home, and she was even more irritated that he went back in. Charmaine met her kids at the top of the stairs.

"You found a book?" She breathed hard due to running up the stairs.

"Yes, we found two!" Morgan smiled, and Charmaine shook her head.

"What did Mommy tell you? I have to do homework, so I can only read one more, but do me a favor, please. Before you come back downstairs, I want you to brush your teeth. Whoever has the whitest teeth will get a prize." She smiled big and wide. It made no sense because she knew her kids would probably eat or drink again before bed. They usually brushed their teeth once they were done eating for the night, but she was desperate for Micha not to see Sammy's face. Kids didn't care about logic. They cared about prizes, and they took off running towards the bathroom. Charmaine skipped back down the steps, ready to slam the door in Sammy's face.

"Get the fuck out of my house!" she hissed and hit him in

the chest when she saw he had the gall to step over the threshold and was actually inside of her home.

Sammy frowned up his face. "Aye, watch your fucking hands now."

He had placed the bags on the couch, and Charmaine picked them up and hurled them outside on the lawn. Sammy rushed out of the house after her. "Are you fucking crazy?" The last thing she wanted was to cause a scene in her nice, quiet, neighborhood, but Sammy had her fucked up.

"Leave. Now. Before I call the police."

Sammy chuckled. "Wow. You really on some other shit. It's all good. I see what I gotta do now." He looked at her like she was really tripping. As if she was the one that had done him wrong in some way.

"Die and go to hell? That's the only thing you could ever do for me!" she snapped before walking back in the house and slamming the door behind her.

Charmaine placed her back against the door and closed her eyes. She really had to take deep breaths in order to compose herself. Had Rico been home, Sammy never would have tried that shit. Charmaine opened her eyes and spotted her phone on the couch. She wished Rico would call her. She really needed to talk to him. He kept his cell phone off for most of the day, but she wondered if she should text it anyway. Charmaine walked over to the couch and sat down. She unlocked her phone and frowned up her face when she saw that he had just called her. She hadn't even heard the phone ring, but why wasn't it a missed call? Charmaine damn near fainted when she went to the call and saw that it had lasted for fifteen seconds. Sammy had answered her fucking phone!

Charmaine was so pissed that tears filled her eyes. She wanted to go find Sammy and put a bullet in his head. Why was he coming around all of a sudden when nobody wanted him to? Hot tears rolled down her cheeks as she tried to call Rico back. She could only imagine what he was thinking. His phone went straight to voicemail just as she heard her kids coming down the stairs, and she quickly wiped her face. Charmaine didn't even have time to cry in peace.

NESHA LOOKED AT CHARMAINE WITH DISBELIEF ALL OVER HER face. "I know you fucking lying! What did he say to Rico?" She shoved a handful of potato chips in her mouth, ready for all the tea Charmaine was spilling.

Charmaine threw her hands up. "I don't know! He hasn't called me since then, and his phone keeps going straight to voicemail. He's pissed. I know it, but Rico has to know that I would never in my life have anything to do with either of my children's sperm donors. Once you do my kids dirty, you don't get second chances with me."

Charmaine almost didn't make it to class that morning, but she knew she had to. School had just started. She couldn't be missing classes already, but she was distraught. Just the thought of Rico being mad at her made her want to throw up. And to make matters worse, every time she tried to call the prison to make a visit, the line was busy. Rico always called her at night before they turned off the phones, and he called when she got out of class. Charmaine had been out of class for an hour and still no Rico. She wanted to cry. In fact, she did cry in the car on the way to Nesha's house. She hated the fact that she couldn't just pick up the phone and call Rico or ride to the prison and see him. Dating a man in prison was some bullshit. Charmaine felt as if she was about to go crazy.

"He's going to call, Charmaine." Nesha tried to comfort her cousin. "Even if he is upset right now, he'll calm down and come to his senses. All the years that Sammy was a deadbeat and did Micha dirty, he has to know that you'd never deal back with that man. You're not even that type of person."

Charmaine shook her head. "I just want to shoot that nigga's mammy's house up. Why would he do that?"

"I know that has to be a rhetorical question. I know you know the answer to that. That loser took one look at the way you came up, and he's hating. He took joy in the fact that you were doing bad with his ass. When you did need his lil' trifling ass fifty dollars a month it made him feel like less of a bum. Now, you have everything he doesn't, and he can't stand the shit. That's some real hating ass shit to do. Sammy is the lamest guy ever for that shit." Nesha couldn't believe he was bitter enough to try and sabotage what Charmaine had going on. "I wish Rico was here to kick his ass. He should be grateful that another man stepped in and has his son living good."

"You wish Rico was here? How do you think I feel? I swear, I don't care if that nigga dies, Nesh." Charmaine really hated Sammy. She loathed him before this situation, but his latest stunt had made it worse. After all she had endured, she deserved to be happy. How dare anyone come and try to mess that up?

Nesha attempted to make Charmaine feel better for a little bit longer, and then she had to go. It was almost time for the kids to get out of school. They went to the same preschool and rode the bus to and from school. Charmaine was going to prepare a quick meal for them because they always got off the school bus acting as if they hadn't eaten all day. As she drove, Charmaine glanced down at the phone in her lap every few minutes. More than anything in this world, she wanted Rico to call her, so she could explain everything to him. He couldn't actually believe that she had been around Sammy by choice. What if he didn't know it was Sammy, and he thought it was another random nigga? She really felt sick. What she wanted at the moment besides to slap Sammy was a glass of wine, but she couldn't have that either. Charmaine's pregnancy test had indeed been positive, and her excitement about it was short lived.

"Please call me," Charmaine wished as she pulled up to her beautiful home. She didn't even have an appetite, but she washed her hands and started cooking for her babies.

An hour later, Charmaine was done and still no call from Rico. When she heard the school bus coming down her street, Charmaine rushed outside and started the walk down the long driveway. By the time she reached the end, Morgan and Micha were running off the bus towards her.

"Hey, babies! How was school?" No matter what she was going through, Charmaine always put on a smile for her children. They began talking a mile a minute while she checked the mail.

Charmaine half-listened as her kids talked over one another in an effort to tell her about their day at school. Charmaine's eyebrows shot up when she saw a letter from the child support office. She hadn't gotten anything from them in a few years, and she stopped going to court long ago. It was nothing but a waste of time to sit in court for hours and only have Sammy be ordered to pay fifty dollars a month, which he didn't even pay. She was over it. As they stepped into the house, Charmaine ripped the letter open. "Go wash your hands, so you can eat," she called out to the kids.

Charmaine scanned the letter, and she jerked her head back when the comprehension of the words on the paper sank in. "This motherfucker is taking me to court for joint custody and child support?!"

Charmaine didn't know whether she wanted to laugh, cry, or have a hit put out on Sammy's bitch ass. She was really over this bullshit!

Chapter TWELVE

"You trying to hit this card game?" James, another inmate, asked Rico as he sat with his arms folded, legs extended in front of him, watching TV in the rec room. He had just finished an intense two-hour workout.

It had been five days since ole boy answered Charmaine's phone. Sleep, exercise, reading, none of it had made Rico's mood any better. He wanted blood. He was trying to change, but the fastest way for him to revert back to the old Rico would be for anybody to try and carry him like a lame ass nigga. Just the thought of Charmaine having that man in the house, fucking and sucking him, and pretending to be a family all off of his work and sacrifice, had him feeling like a real sucker. All the OG's in prison always warned that you can't trust no bitch on the outside. But he really felt like Charmaine was different. His heart wanted to believe there was another reason, but his mind kept telling him the nigga wasn't at the house for nothing, and he felt comfortable enough to answer her phone. He wish he was home, he'd make that bitch ass nigga with all the mouth swallow his teeth.

"Nope, I'm good," Rico replied gruffly while never taking his eyes off the TV screen. He didn't want to be bothered. When Rico was in a foul mood, it was best for him to stay away from people.

Now that a few days had passed, he was even angrier that he broke the phone that he paid three-hundred dollars to have smuggled in to him. A lot of inmates had cell phones, but the process of getting one wasn't an easy one at all, and a good number of people got caught trying to sneak them in.

Rico didn't fuck with many, but the ones he did talk to had seen a change in his behavior and mood. They were all in the same situation, and they knew enough to know that something must be going on, on the outside. It happened to all inmates at some point. It was too easy in prison to get some bad news over the phone or in a letter that would fuck up an inmate's day.

Candice, the correctional officer that had slid him the number when he was leaving the first time, came over to Rico. She studied him for a bit, wondering if she should say anything to his mean looking ass. "I see you put in a request to take your lady friend's name off your visitation list. You sure that's what you want to do? She just called again and tried to schedule a visit for next week."

Rico looked over at her slowly. "If I wasn't sure about wanting it off, I wouldn't have put the request in."

Candice held her hands up in surrender. " Oh, let me just go back to my corner and mind my business."

"That would be nice," Rico grumbled as his eyes went back to the television screen.

Candice sucked her teeth and walked off. The lowkey hater in her couldn't help but smirk. When he got out, he didn't hit her up because he was so busy making sure his girl had a great

Christmas. Seems like he went above and beyond for her and was ready to do right by her, and she messed it up. Some dumb females were on the outside being faithful for months and years to men that weren't shit and weren't ever going to be shit. But a lot of these females out there had as much game as the men. They were playing the good girl role while doing their thing every night with some dick that was out in the free world. Rico seemed like a smart man, so if Charmaine was out there doing dirt, she wondered why he was even surprised. It wasn't her business though. Maybe since there was trouble in paradise, when he got out in six months, he would give her a call.

Candice wasn't in the mood to give up since she knew that Rico and his girl were on the outs. She watched him when he got up and walked out of the rec room. Candice waited a few minutes before she walked out of the room as well. A lot of the inmates were about to head to eat dinner, but Rico rarely ever went to the cafeteria. He always had money on his books, so he bought most of his food from the canteen and cooked his own meals. He always got soup, chicken, noodles, rice, chips, candy, ice cream, etc. Rico ate like a king in prison. Candice had never seen him eat from the cafeteria in all the time she had been working there. She felt it was now or never since there were less pairs of eyes around.

Candice stood at the door of his cell. "Nichols, come with me to the laundry room." Candice had been working at the prison long enough to know where all the blind spots were or the areas that couldn't be viewed on the surveillance cameras. There weren't many of them, but there were enough.

Rico followed Candice, curiously wondering what she wanted with him. He really wasn't in the mood to be doing anything other than reading until he fell asleep. He didn't need any laundry done, and he for damn sure wasn't about to be doing anyone else's. When they made it inside the room,

Candice led him over to a corner. She started massaging his dick through his pants while she gazed into his eyes.

"It looks like you need some stress relief."

Her actions confused Rico, but as his dick started to harden, he didn't feel the need to stop her. Candice took it a step further and reached inside his pants. Rico was so shocked, he couldn't speak. The way his eyes were half-closed had her wanting to really blow his mind by giving him head, but she couldn't do all that at work. Had he called and linked with her, he might know what her head game was like by now.

"I just want you to feel better," she purred, and he almost moaned at the way her soft hand felt slowly jacking his dick. It was nowhere near close to the feeling of pussy, but it damn sure felt good.

It had been weeks, shit, almost a month since him and Charmaine had sex. Rico hadn't even masturbated since he'd been back in prison, so he wasn't complaining at the pleasure that Candice was giving him. Being that he was pissed with Charmaine, and felt like she was out there fucking her baby daddy, he didn't even have to feel guilty about the hand job that he was receiving. Candice knew she needed to hurry up, so she got on some freaky shit and started moaning and licking her lips as she stroked him faster.

"Damn, I want to swallow all this cum up. I bet it tastes like candy," she talked dirty to him. "It would be even better if you came all up in this fat pussy. It's so tight, baby. I haven't had sex in almost a year."

Ordinarily, Rico would have never cum that fast from a hand job, but he was backed up, and Candice's lil' freaky ass was turning him on. When his breathing became shallow, she changed her mind about not sucking him off and deep throated him. That would be the best way to make sure there was no mess left behind to clean up. Rico stared down at the top of her head with his mouth hanging open. Shorty was definitely full of surprises, and he wasn't complaining.

"What was that about?" he asked after he shot a load down her throat, and she swallowed it up.

Candice simply smirked. "I'm not asking you again to call me once you're out next time. If you decide not to, that's on you. I just decided to give you a little preview."

Rico went back to his cell feeling light as a feather. He had women out here damn near begging for some of his time and attention. He felt that he had a right to be upset by Charmaine's betrayal, but he knew once he was over it, he'd be over it for good. When he was released, he was going to move on with his life.

CHARMAINE WATCHED AS THE NURSE GAVE MS. MARY HER medication. When the nurse was done tending to the older woman, she walked out of the room, and Charmaine looked down at her watch. Nesha was watching her kids while she came to visit Rico's grandmother in the hospital. God truly worked in mysterious ways because one of Ms. Mary's grand-children had reached out to Charmaine via social media and told her that the lady had suffered a mild stroke. She had been in the hospital for three days, and she wanted to speak with Charmaine. Rico's cousin followed him on Facebook, and she found Charmaine that way, even though Rico never posted. Charmaine wasted no time coming to see what the woman wanted to see her about. So far, it hadn't been anything impera-tive, but she still enjoyed talking with her.

"Ms. Mary, is there anything that you want me to do before I go?" In the three hours that she sat with Ms. Mary, Charmaine had told her a lot. The woman had a comforting spirit about her even after she had gone through what she did. Charmaine did most of the talking, but Ms. Mary seemed to be in good spirits.

She was even able to tell Charmaine stories about Rico's childhood, and most of them made her laugh. Ms. Mary's speech was a little slow, and she would need physical therapy for her left side, but it wasn't as bad as it could have been. The doctors said she might've been able to go home in three or four days. Charmaine planned to come see her every day. Before Ms. Mary could answer her, the phone in her room rang, and Charmaine got up to get it, so she wouldn't have to reach for it. She passed the phone to Ms. Mary.

"Hello? Baby calm down, I'm fine, Rico. It was just a mild stroke."

Charmaine's knees buckled. Rico was on the phone?! She held her breath as she tried to hear over the pounding of her heart.

Ms. Mary continued, "It wasn't as bad as it could have been. The doctors are hopeful that I can go home in three or four days. Don't you worry, just pray, I'll be fine. Now if you want to do something for me, I need you to speak with Charmaine and you hear her out."

Charmaine's eyes widened as Ms. Mary passed her the phone. She swallowed hard and clutched the phone in her hand. "Hello?"

"What are you doing there?" he asked in a gruff voice. It hurt her that he sounded like she was the last person that he ever wanted to talk to, all because of a misunderstanding.

"Rico, I know you're pissed, but just listen to me. I had my old car towed to my mother's house and the bast—" Not wanting to disrespect Ms. Mary, Charmaine stopped herself from calling Sammy ungodly names. "The guy that towed the car is Micha's dad's cousin. He told him where I live, and Sammy showed up with all these gifts asking to see Micha. I wasn't letting that happen, so when I heard Micha at the top of the steps, I ran upstairs to stop him. I knew if he saw Sammy, he'd want him to come in, and I wasn't letting that happen. I convinced the kids to brush their teeth. When I came back downstairs, I saw that he was inside the house, and I took all the gifts and tossed them outside and made him get out. I had no idea that he answered my phone until I tried to text you." Her voice cracked, and Rico's heart melted when he realized she was on the verge of tears. He had really been about to cut her off from his life over nothing. Rico was angry and hurt all over again but for a different reason this time.

"Babe, I'm so fucking sorry," he stated in a low tone. All he wanted to do at that moment was beat Sammy's ass. After that, he wanted to hug his girl and apologize over and over again.

"That's not even the worst part. I got custody papers in the mail. He wants joint custody and child support from me! Things have just been going so wrong. I needed to talk to you so badly."

Charmaine sounded so sad; Rico hated himself for how he'd treated her. He should have been a man and let her explain no matter how bad the situation had seemed. "I'm so sorry. I'm gon' handle this shit for you. Somehow, someway. And I'm putting your name back on my list. Please forgive me."

"I just wanted you to know what was up, but I can't even make this about me right now. Your cousin, Patrice, reached out to me. Your grandmother wanted to see me. We met when I went to her church and kind of spoke to her on your behalf."

All Rico could do was smile. She had done that for him? "Yeah, I was wondering how the chaplain knew that she had a stroke, but the nurse from the hospital called up here and asked them to tell me. Seems my grandma asked her to do so, and I have you to thank for that. I love you, Charmaine. I love you, and I'm so sorry. They're telling me I gotta go. Tell my grandma I love her too."

"I will, baby. I love you too."

Charmaine hung up the phone and looked over at Ms. Mary with a wide smile. "You did that for me?"

"I felt sorry for you, so when you went to get something to eat, I asked the nurse to call. I initially asked you up here because when I was laying on the floor in my kitchen thinking I was about to die, and all I saw was Rico's face. I even heard his voice clear as day telling me he was sorry. I felt like God was telling me that I needed to make things right with him. I never stopped loving Rico, but I was some kind of hot with him, and I can be stubborn as a mule. It wasn't a good feeling though to think I might be dying, and the last time I talked to the boy I raised was nearly five years ago. I just couldn't continue on without talking to him. To me, that would be too much like not appreciating the second chance that God gave me. But when you got here looking all sad and told me what happened, I decided that for now, you needed to talk to him more than me. I will talk to Rico in due time."

Charmaine smiled wider. "Thank you so much. Lord knows I've been stressing. Your grandson is stubborn too, and he was not messing with me. I feel so much better having heard his voice. You really made my day. Even after you go home, I'll come by and help you whenever you need me to. Thank you so much for your help."

Ms. Mary chuckled. "Child, don't say thank you nan other time. I just did what I felt was right. You want to thank me? Do it by sitting that grandson of mine down and letting him know that you won't tolerate no foolishness out of him. I love Rico, and I will forgive him. I'll even tell him that I forgive him, but it's still going to take a lot of prayer for me to get all the way over what he did. He hurt innocent people, and I just..." Ms. Mary shook her head. "I'm not even going to think about it. But please do what I said. Let Rico know you will not accept no mess. Not even one time."

"I will certainly do that."

Visiting hours were coming to an end, and Charmaine left the hospital feeling better than she had in days. She was still sweating bullets just thinking about the latest stunt that Sammy had pulled, but she felt a little better knowing that she didn't have to deal with it alone.

Chapter THIRTEEN

Charmaine looked on nervously as the lawyer looked over the papers that she brought into the office with her. That morning, Lauren had deposited $2,800 in her account. The $2,800 was profit, and her initial investment of $10,000 had been reinvested. Charmaine wanted to be able to get a lawyer, and she didn't want to have to use Rico's money or any of her savings to do so. She really felt that it was unnecessary. The shit that Sammy was doing was so trifling. Charmaine needed that money to fall back on. She was doing a good job of saving it and not blowing through it. She would be damned if she let Sammy get his slimy hands on any of it.

The middle-aged white woman with long, blonde hair looked up at Charmaine. "It says here that the child's father wants joint custody of the child, and he wants child support from you, so that he can provide the child with the same lifestyle at his home that the child has at yours. Where do you work?"

"I don't work. The house that I live in, and the car that I drive were purchased by my boyfriend. He takes care of me. I'm in school. I've barely even lived in that house for a month. Before that, I lived with my mother. Before that, I lived in low-income housing." Charmaine wasn't telling her about the money she had in the bank unless she absolutely had to.

"What is the current visitation schedule?"

"There isn't one. Sammy isn't active in his son's life. A few weeks ago was his first time attempting to visit his son in months. He's thousands of dollars in arrears because he doesn't even pay the fifty dollars a month child support he's supposed to. Sammy is a deadbeat that only sees dollar signs. He left me struggling with my son for years, and he didn't even try to help. Now, he wants money from me?" Charmaine was the type that cried when she was angry, and she was on the verge of tears for sure because she was pissed just talking about Sammy's trifling ass.

"Trust me when I tell you that no judge in his or her right mind would grant your son's father joint custody. He doesn't work, and where does he live?"

"With his mother."

"The motive for this filing is clear. Your son's father doesn't have a leg to stand on, and you shouldn't be worried at all. Besides, if you don't work, you wouldn't be ordered to pay more than him which would be fifty dollars a month. You and your boyfriend aren't married, so his income can't be used in court. Sammy has no case."

Charmaine exhaled a sigh of relief. "Oh my God, thank you so much."

"It's my pleasure. One of the reasons that I love my job is because I want all deadbeat parents to have to be held account-able. Children are innocent, and they shouldn't suffer because one or both parents are immature. It would be a pleasure for me to represent you and tear this man to shreds in court."

Charmaine couldn't stop smiling. Things were starting to look up again for her. She just had one more thing she needed done, and money wasn't an issue. "I know you're a family lawyer, but maybe you can point me in the right direction of someone that can help me."

SAMMY PULLED UP AT HIS MOTHER'S HOUSE AND GOT OUT OF THE car. It was one in the morning, and he was pissed the fuck off. He had only made two hundred dollars that day selling drugs, and he had lost all of that but five dollars gambling. He was sick. Not only was he broke, but he was $180 short on his re-up, so until he got that money, he wouldn't be getting any more drugs. Foolishly, he hit the card table, hoping to turn his two hundred dollars into five hundred. When he first started, he was on a winning streak. He won seventy-five, and he should have just gotten up and left then, but he didn't, and now he had a new dilemma on his hands.

Sammy had never been so ready to go to court in his life. He needed Charmaine's big ballin' ass to be ordered to pay him a few hundred dollars a month in child support. He had spent an hour stalking her Instagram page and in the past month, she'd been posted up in Louis, Gucci, and Chanel. Micha and Morgan had even taken professional pictures dressed in Burberry. He was hating for sure, but even though he was a grimy nigga, he refused to run up in there and rob her while his son was there. That was too savage even for him. He didn't want his son to end up traumatized from witnessing a home invasion.

Sammy let other people that didn't know shit just like he didn't, tell him that Charmaine could pay him child support since her nigga had so much money. No one gave him accurate advice, and he wasn't smart enough to research it on his own. If Charmaine didn't work and her nigga wasn't her husband, it didn't matter how good she was living. The judge couldn't order her to pay him just because she was living good. It wasn't that Sammy didn't love his son, but he didn't have a father, therefore, he didn't know how to be one.

Sammy had only taken three steps when he felt a blow to the back of the head so hard that he stumbled forward and fell on his face. His nose cracked as it made contact with the ground, and he groaned in pain. Between the burning in his nose and the pounding in his head, Sammy had never felt that much pain in his life, and it wasn't over. Someone stomped him in the back so hard, he lost control of his bladder. He would have sworn his spine was broken in half if he couldn't still feel his legs.

"Please," he croaked as the person attacking him turned his body over.

His pleas went ignored as the assailant punched him in the face over and over again. By the fourth blow, Sammy could no longer feel his nose, and it felt like he was choking on his own blood. A strong hand wrapped around his neck and choked him until his eyes began to roll back in his head.

"Stay the fuck away from Charmaine," he heard as he began to feel light headed.

The man choking him let Sammy's neck go, and he gasped for air while gurgling blood. Sammy scrambled to get up off the ground, and that wasn't easy to do when every inch of his body literally hurt. He hated to even go in the house like that, and he prayed that his mother was asleep. He had seen pictures of Charmaine's man on her page, and he did some digging. The nigga was locked up, so he must have sent one of his goons after him, Sammy thought. He was going to have to take a shower and go to the ER for his broken nose. Charmaine didn't have brothers. It could have been a cousin or somebody, but he had a feeling it was someone Rico sent. To Sammy, this further proved that Rico had money and reach. If Charmaine had a cousin or something that wanted to ride for her, they would have been whooped his ass long ago. This was all Rico, and Sammy was gon' get that ass one way or another. Somebody had to pay for this and if he couldn't get at Rico, then he'd take the shit out on Charmaine.

Chapter
FOURTEEN

R ico squeezed Charmaine's hand as she sat at the table across from him. "I've been trying to let my grandma get her rest, so I haven't called her since she's been home. I want to thank you though. Going to church to talk to her really lets me know how down you are for me. And how crazy you are 'cus on a bad day, Mary would have whooped yo' ass."

Charmaine laughed. "Trust me when I tell you, I was shaking like a stripper. She looks like she doesn't play. She wasn't rude, but she wasn't thinking about what I was talking about that day. It touched her though, and having a stroke is what did it. She doesn't want to die with you two being on bad terms."

Rico looked away and stared at the wall for a bit. Just the thought of her dying had him fighting back tears. Mary was his heart. The fact that they lost so much time because of the stupid shit he did would always bother him. He prayed that his grandmother had more years left in her. He just couldn't lose her anytime soon. That shit would devastate him. It was Charmaine's turn to squeeze Rico's hand, and he stared into her eyes.

"How have you been though? That pussy ass nigga been back around you?" Rico chose not to tell her that he'd paid someone $1500 to beat Sammy's ass since he couldn't do it himself. He also had to deal with the guilt he felt every time he looked into her face. Rico didn't have sex with Candice, but she had her hands and her mouth on his dick. Charmaine wouldn't appreciate that shit, and Rico was disappointed in himself that he didn't stop her. Being hurt and pissed and not thinking straight had him doing things he shouldn't have been doing, and he was sorry. Since he found out that Sammy showed up at the crib, he'd been worried that the nigga would be a problem for Charmaine.

"No, I haven't heard from him thank God. I hope he just decides to leave me alone." Charmaine felt Rico tense up.

"That muhfucka is *going* to leave you alone."

Charmaine didn't like the look in his eyes, and it wasn't because she didn't want him to harm Sammy. Lowkey, she wanted Sammy's ass to suffer, but it wasn't worth her man getting into trouble. She rubbed the back of his hand. "Babe, it's not even worth it. The lawyer already told me that he doesn't have a case. Filing the papers, going to court, all that is just a waste of his time. He's a dumb ass."

"When is the court date?"

"In like five weeks. The nigga was trying to get a closer date. He really thinks that he's going to walk in that courtroom and be awarded some money. He has to be on drugs. He has to be." She shook her head.

"I wish I was there to go with you."

"You might be." She smiled, confusing Rico.

"You said five weeks. You meant five months?" he asked with a puzzled expression on his face.

Charmaine smiled wider. "It would be better if it could be a surprise, but the lawyer has to meet with you. The family attorney recommended a lawyer to me that may be able to expedite your release. Now, if you get out before the five months are up, you won't be on parole, but you will have to be on house arrest. I know you wanted to come home and be free and clear but baby, being in the house with me and the kids won't be so bad, will it?"

She looked so hopeful and excited that he had to grin. "No, that won't be bad at all. How much did that shit cost?"

"A lot. But you're worth it. We can exercise together, you can study for your CDL, I'll cook for you every night. We can have movie nights. I can't wait. He told me he can't give me a release date just yet, but he's hopeful he can get it done in less than thirty days."

"Wow, this shit is crazy." Rico shook his head because he was really speechless. No one had ever gone so hard for him. First, she reached out to his grandmother on his behalf, and now she had gone to see a lawyer about getting him out. Through his peripheral vision, he saw Candice enter the visitation room, and he shifted in his seat. Every time he saw her face, he was reminded of how he had betrayed Charmaine.

"With everything you've done for me, I had to. You committed a nonviolent crime, you've done more than eighty percent of your time, covid is running rampant, and you'd be in the house. Why not let you out? You were already released once, and your crazy ass came back."

"I know. I've been regretting that shit too. Especially after my grandmother had that stroke. I've been kicking myself in the ass."

"It's almost over for good this time. I promise you. Once you leave here, that will be it forever."

"Damn right it will be."

The visit flew by as they normally did and when it was over, Charmaine hated to go. She really hoped that Rico would be home before January was over. It would be absolutely perfect if he was home by Valentine's Day. She had something great planned for them if he was home but even if he wasn't, she planned to visit him that day and tell him about her pregnancy. It was hard hiding it from him, but she wanted the way she told him to be romantic. Charmaine had her first doctor's appointment the day before, and she was relieved when she heard the baby's heartbeat. This pregnancy was so unlike her other two. She hadn't had any symptoms and was beginning to think something was wrong. Charmaine wasn't a big ice cream eater, and lately, she wanted ice cream every day. Aside from that, there was no throwing up, no feeling nauseous, she didn't feel pregnant at all. But at her visit, she had been assured that everything looked good. Charmaine couldn't wait to see the look on Rico's face when she told him she was pregnant. That would be the best Valentine's Day ever.

As Rico and the other inmates filed out of the visitation room, he ignored the feel of Candice's eyes on him. He hoped she wasn't about to start that weird shit. He didn't ask her to do what she did that day in the laundry room. That had been all her. She found out that he was mad with Charmaine, and she used it to her advantage. Rico had never sold her any dreams or made her any promises. Out of all the inmates in the prison that flirted with her daily and gassed her like she was the baddest female on earth, Rico didn't need her focusing on him. Now, he was glad that his phone was broken. A salty female couldn't be underestimated, and he didn't need her doing anything to try and get him in trouble.

Rico was starving, so he warmed up some soup and was about to sit down and eat it, when she made her way over to him. "That was the shortest fucking breakup in history."

"Why are you keeping track though? My relationship and its issues should be none of your concern. I love my girl, and I've never said otherwise."

Candice gave him a look that could kill, and she had to remember where she was to keep from going off on him. He was right. He didn't speak to her about his relationship. She knew he was getting out soon, and she was desperate to get his attention. The many inmates in the prison may have been on her, but Candice didn't get attention in the outside world like she got at work. To those horny pussy deprived men, she may as well have been Cardi B. Out in the world, she was a regular woman with a super fat ass. Men tried her, but she hadn't had a man as fine as Rico try to get at her in years. His handsome face, his muscular physique, his cocky demeanor made her pussy cream. She liked how he didn't act thirsty for her but in turn, she acted thirsty for him, and she had played herself. Rico had shown her once again that he really did love his woman. All Candice could do was take her L, but she didn't have to be happy about it.

"Watch how you talk to me, inmate!" she snapped at him and walked off.

All Rico could do was chuckle. That broad was certified crazy.

TEN DAYS LATER, RICO WAS ONCE AGAIN WALKING OUT OF PRISON a free man. All he could do was smile when he saw Charmaine hopping out of the Range Rover he had copped her. She ran and jumped into her man's arms and planted kisses all over his face. "I see you're happy to see a nigga." He laughed.

"You have no idea. I am so freaking happy. And you're driving!" She kissed him one more time and hopped out of his arms.

Rico didn't have a problem with that. He was ready to get behind the wheel of a car. He needed to work on getting his own transportation under control. He still wasn't broke by far, but if he wanted to buy his own truck, he didn't need to go out and buy himself a super expensive luxury car like he'd gotten Charmaine. As long as he was mobile, it didn't have to be anything extravagant for now. Rico had the most important thing; a nice place to live. To him, that was more important than stuntin' in exotic cars. His thirst for fast cash and flashy material items were what landed him in prison in the first place. He was determined to come home with a different mindset.

"I already told the kids about you. They've never lived with a man before, but I hope it will be an easy adjustment for all of us."

Rico reached over and grabbed her hand. "I'm sure it will be."

During the car ride, the couple talked about all of their plans for the future. Rico had to go straight home. They didn't even have to stop for food because Charmaine had cooked for him. The kids were still in school, so they had the house to themselves for three more hours. As soon as they walked in the house, the aroma of food filled Rico's nostrils. "I got up at five this morning and started cooking. We have beef ribs, garlic mashed potatoes, grilled zucchini, and cornbread."

Rico pulled Charmaine into his arms for a big bear hug. "Have I ever told you that I love you?"

She smiled as she looked up at her man. "Yes, you have. Plenty of times, and I love you too."

Rico's tongue invaded her mouth, and the lovers kissed passionately in the middle of the kitchen. "This food smells amazing but before I dig in, I want to take a shower, then eat you," he stated seriously.

"That sounds like a plan to me." Charmaine grabbed Rico's

hand and led him up the stairs. In the bedroom, he looked at all of the items she had sprawled out on the bed. Versace pajama pants, Versace boxer briefs, and matching bedroom shoes. There was also a white tank top, a Versace robe, a toothbrush, lotion, cologne, and Polo socks. There were also Polo sweat suits in three different colors. "Just because you have to be confined to the house doesn't mean you can't be fly."

Rico pulled Charmaine into his arms for another hug. He had never purchased a woman a house or a Range, but when he was committing fraud, he bought women plenty of things. He'd purchased designer bags, jewelry, clothes, and shoes. He'd even taken women on trips, and as soon as he got locked up, every last one of them bailed on him. He had to think long and hard about whether or not he was playing himself to set Charmaine up the way that he did, and it was a huge relief for him that he hadn't played himself. She was riding with him hard as hell, proving that he made the right choice by upgrading her life. Rico's dick was getting hard from their bodies being pressed together, so he pulled back and kissed her on the forehead.

"Thank you, baby. I'm about to hop in the shower and wash these prison germs off me."

As soon as he went into the bathroom, Charmaine grabbed her small bag and headed for the bathroom the kids mostly used. She took a quick shower as well and when she was done, she put on Rico's favorite lotion and perfume. It smelled different to her since she was pregnant, but she hoped it still smelled the same to him. Charmaine was trying to get nasty, so she didn't care about getting too cute. She brushed her long weave up into a high ponytail and stepped into the red, lace, one piece lingerie set that she'd purchased. Charmaine wasn't even self-conscious about her slight pudge or her small love handles. Rico made her feel just that secure. She wanted to beat him out of the bathroom, so Charmaine checked her appearance and rushed back into the bedroom. The shower had stopped, but Rico was still in the bathroom.

Charmaine got on the bed and posed in the sexiest position that didn't make her feel like she looked stupid. She was nervous and excited for what was to come and when the bathroom door opened, her heart started to beat a little faster.

"Damn," Rico marveled when he saw her on the bed. "You look good as fuck."

He had the Versace boxer briefs on for all of two minutes before he was pulling them back off. He pulled Charmaine to the edge of the bed, placed his face between her legs, and pulled her lingerie to the side. Rico stared at her mound for a few seconds before separating her slit with his tongue. He gave a few slow licks, then he pulled her clitoris into his mouth and sucked softly. Charmaine closed her eyes and moaned as he treated her pussy like it was a piece of candy. Rico alternated between sucking and licking. By the time he slid one finger into her while he flicked his tongue over her love button, Charmaine was calling his name and gripping the back of her head as she came.

Rico's eyes lifted, and he peered at her face, making sure she was completely satisfied. Knowing that her clit was sensitive after an orgasm, he moved over and started sucking on the inside of her thighs. Rico wanted to get her off because he would cum very quick his first time. It didn't matter though because he would be tearing that ass up every day while the kids were in school and every night. Rico used his tongue to place a trail from her belly to her breasts. He took her right nipple into his mouth and sucked on it until Charmaine squirmed underneath him. She wanted penetration. By the time their lips connected, she was so ready for the dick that she grabbed it and inserted it herself. Rico moaned at how warm, wet, and tight her pussy was. He doubted he'd even last ten good strokes.

Rico broke the kiss, so he could look down and admire Charmaine's body while he rocked in and out of her. There could be no more messing up on his part. Other women, illegal money, all of that was a wrap. All he wanted to do was make her as happy as she'd made him. Rico lasted longer than he thought he would, but he was still ready to erupt rather quickly.

"I'm about to cum all up in this pussy, mami," he moaned as she clenched her pussy muscles and gripped his dick like a vice.

"I'm about to cum with you, baby." Charmaine cupped her sensitive breasts in her hands and let out a loud groan as she exploded at the same time as Rico.

He kissed her before rolling off of her. "That was fucking amazing."

"It was, wasn't it?"

"Now, a nigga's stomach is growling."

Charmaine sat up and scooted off the bed. "Let me clean up, throw some clothes on, and fix your plate. The kids will be home soon, so we can go for round two later on tonight."

"I look forward to it." Rico watched her ass as she walked away from him. A nigga was finally home, and he was home to stay this time.

Outside of their home, Sammy sat across the street lurking. He had already been there for four hours, and he needed to leave before someone called the police. This wasn't the kind of neighborhood you wanted to be spotted in for not belonging. Sammy pulled up on Charmaine's street twenty minutes before she left out. It had only been a week since he got his ass beat, and his face was still fucked up. He had a splint on his nose, his left eye was an ugly shade of purple, and his back was still fucked up. Sammy needed strong pain killers just to sleep at night. He was embarrassed every time someone saw his face and reacted like he was the most gruesome sight ever. He made up a story about getting jumped and robbed but people that really knew him didn't believe that tale. Sammy was broke as hell. Who would waste time trying to rob him?

He was determined to make Charmaine pay for what her nigga had done to him, but imagine his surprise when she pulled back up two hours later with the nigga in the car. Her nigga was finally home. Now, Sammy could start plotting for real.

Chapter
FIFTEEN

Charmaine looked over at Rico. "Are you nervous?"

"I'd be lying if I said I wasn't. It will be my first time being in the same room with my grandmother in a long time."

"You know she's coming over after a physical therapy session, and she's probably tired. Don't feel bad if she doesn't stay long." Rico could tell that Charmaine was worried about how the reunion would go, and her main concern was Rico not feeling disappointed or rejected.

"I know, babe. If it wasn't for this ankle monitor, I'd go see her."

The doorbell rang, and Rico swallowed what felt like a lump. Charmaine let him get up and answer the door and as soon as his grandmother and cousin, Patrice, stepped inside the house, Rico hugged her tight. Charmaine's eyes widened a bit because she thought he might be handling her a little too rough, since she only stood about 5'4 and had just had a stroke. The two stayed in their embrace for a good while and when Charmaine realized that the both of them were crying, tears filled her eyes as well. The fact that Ms. Mary was willing to forgive Rico was going to make him so happy, and Charmaine loved that for him.

Finally, Rico and Ms. Mary pulled apart, and he grabbed her hand and led her to the couch. "This is a beautiful home. I hope you went about getting it the right way." Ms. Mary was a straight shooter. She might've forgiven Rico, but that didn't mean she was going to bite her tongue or not be true to who she was.

"I'm not running after fast money anymore, Grandma. I'm about to start truck driving school, and I'm going to get my own truck. Charmaine is in school too. I wasted a lot of time in prison. I'm not wasting anymore. You raised me better than how I acted, and I will forever regret hurting you and other innocent people. I've asked God for forgiveness several times."

"You only have to ask him once. After He forgives you, it doesn't matter who else doesn't. I'm human, so it took me some time. I worship God, but I'm far from perfect, and I can hold a mean grudge. Life is short though, and it was time for me to get over what happened. It's done, and it can't be taken back. If it changed you for the better, then it was a necessary evil."

Ms. Mary and her grandson chatted for about an hour, and then she was exhausted. She did promise to come back for Sunday dinner. When she left, Rico looked at the time and saw that they had an hour before the kids got home. "I'm about to eat that pussy. Take these pants off." He tugged at her sweatpants, and she laughed.

"I'm never turning down any head." Charmaine laughed

She straddled her man's lap, and they kissed passionately. Charmaine grinded on his lap as they kissed, and he placed his hands underneath her shirt and fondled her breasts. A loud bang caused them both to jump, and Rico's street instincts kicked in. Since it was daytime and the kids would be in soon, they didn't set the alarm after Ms. Mary and Patrice left. It could be the police, or it could be jack boys. It was better to be safe than sorry. Rico tossed Charmaine off his lap as another loud bang came from the front door.

"Run upstairs and get the strap."

Just as Charmaine dashed towards the steps, another loud bang sent the front door flying open. Rico felt like a sitting duck as he jumped up off the couch. He was fresh out of prison, on house arrest, and not planning to be out in the streets. Rico knew that trouble could find anybody, so he planned to get a strap eventually but since his girl had one, he wasn't pressed. Who would be running up in his shit out in the suburbs in the middle of the day?

"Take me to the money, nigga," a gruff voice demanded.

Rico looked at the man's ski masked covered face with a scowl. All of the money he had was tied up in investments. Since being home, he hadn't spoken to Lauren about withdrawing anything. He didn't have a dollar in his pocket. Everything he needed was in the house, and Charmaine's money was in the bank. Rico held his hands up in surrender.

"Nigga, I'm fresh out of prison. I don't have any money in the house. My girl is here, and our kids are on the way home. We don't have shit," Rico spoke slowly.

It burned Sammy up to hear Rico refer to the kids as his. This nigga really was trying to completely take over as Micha's dad, and Charmaine's hoe ass was letting him just because he had money.

"Nigga, you got something, and if you don't take me to it, I'm putting lead in your ass." He was going to do that anyway since Rico had him beaten. But he wanted the money first. They had something in that bitch, and he wasn't leaving without it.

Charmaine crept down the steps as quietly as she could.

She wanted to catch the intruder by surprise, but her heart was beating so loudly, she was sure he would be able to hear it. She prayed that it was just one of them because she doubted she'd be able to take two of them. She held her breath, pointed the gun at the intruder, and squeezed the trigger before he had time to react. The man howled from the pain and gripped his shoulder where the bullet had entered his body. Rico used that chance to rush the man and slam his body into the wall. He punched him in the face and ripped the ski mask off. Charmaine gasped.

"Sammy?! You really ran up in my fucking house, you sorry ass bitch?" She ran over to him and hit him in the face with the butt of the gun. She was so tired of his ass, she didn't know what to do and for a brief second, and killing him really entered her mind. All of the problems he was causing her made no sense and for what?

"You two stupid muhfuckas get off me." Sammy was ready to shit himself when the butt of the gun connected with his already broken nose. His shoulder was on fire, and he was scared out of his mind.

"Nigga, you in my house!" Rico roared. "I never thought I'd see the day that I fucked with the police, but you aren't jeopardizing my freedom. I'm on house arrest, and I'm not risking shit. Your ass going to jail is the best way to ensure that you stay away from Charmaine and Micha. Because I'm really close to killing you, and I'm trying to change my life." Rico looked over at Charmaine. "Baby, see if Nesha can come get the kids off the bus, so they won't have to come in and see this sorry ass piece of shit bleeding on our floor. Then, call the police and tell them that someone broke into our house."

Sammy's eyes widened. "No, man. You can't do that shit. Come on, you a street nigga. How you gonna call the fucking police on me?" Sammy was on the verge of tears.

"Were you sticking to the G-code when you took out child

support papers on Charmaine, huh nigga? You want me to stick to the street code and kill you? You'd rather die than go to prison? Because there is no way in hell that I'm letting you walk up out of this house." Just thinking about all of Sammy's antics had Rico livid, and he punched the man in the face just because. "Fuck ass nigga gon' kick in my door?" he breathed hard as he hit Rico again and blood flew from his mouth onto the white wall. "You in here fucking up my walls and floors with your blood and shit." He hit him again and that time, Sammy did start crying.

He had messed all the way up, and there was no coming back from it. Before Charmaine could even get off the phone with Nesha, police sirens blared, and three cars raced onto the street and pulled up in the driveway. "You thought you could kick in this door in broad daylight in this neighborhood? Dumb ass." Rico shook his head.

He didn't want to have to deal with the police, and he was going to let Charmaine do most of the talking. It was her gun, her baby daddy, and she had shot the nigga. Rico was just a witness. The police ran into the house with their weapons drawn, and Rico and Charmaine put their hands up in the air while Sammy was on the verge of passing out.

Chapter SIXTEEN

Charmaine dropped the sponge that she was holding, ran to the bathroom, and threw up. The police had questioned her and Rico for about an hour and thirty minutes after they put Sammy in the back of an ambulance and handcuffed him to the gurney. They eventually told her that no charges would be filed against her, and they left. Rico was pissed as he called one of his homeboys and asked him to go to Home Depot and get him an entire front door, since he couldn't leave the house. Sammy had fucked the door up to where it couldn't even be closed all the way, and it was too cold outside for all of that. All of the drama from the day coupled with the gore and the stench of the blood made Charmaine nauseous. As she was flushing the toilet Rico entered the bathroom.

"Are you okay?"

Charmaine looked at him and started crying. "I was trying

to wait until Valentine's Day to tell you, but that's still almost a week away. I'm just over all the drama and all the bullshit. I just want to be happy. I'm pregnant," she sobbed.

"What?" Rico asked dumbfounded as he pulled her into his arms.

"I've known for a few weeks. I wanted to surprise you for Valentine's Day. I just wanted that day to be extra special."

"Yo, I want you off your feet now. Go take a shower and get in the bed. I'll worry about the door and clean the house up. I'll also give Nesha some bread to bring the kids home, so you don't have to go out."

"No, Rico. You don't have to treat me like I'm handicapped. I don't have any morning sickness or anything. Today is the first time I've thrown up, and it was the smell of the blood. I'm okay." She wiped her tears away, but Rico wasn't having it.

"You just went through a lot. Today was traumatizing. If you stress too much and something happens, I will forget all about changing and kill Sammy myself. I got this. Go relax."

Charmaine nodded and peeled her clothes off, so she could get in the shower. It had been a long, traumatizing day indeed. She didn't know what in the world had gotten into Sammy. That man actually kicked her door in and tried to rob them. He had a gun and everything. Charmaine recalled the bruises on his face and wondered what had happened. She didn't really care. In the event that he was able to post bond, she hoped that he would just mind his damn business. Her being with a good man bothered Sammy so much that he ruined his own life bothering her. That was some sick and twisted shit. What if Micha had been home? She shivered at the thought. This was too damn much, and she was going to take Rico's advice. After a long, hot shower, she was going to eat something, then curl up in bed. Charmaine had been through enough drama to last a lifetime.

❄

THE NEXT DAY, THE BLOOD WAS ALL CLEANED UP, THE DOOR WAS fixed, and Rico waited on Charmaine hand and foot. It was the weekend, so she didn't have class. He made her breakfast in bed, played Xbox with the kids, did laundry, and ordered them take-out for lunch, and they watched movies. The kids had never had a father figure, so they were loving Rico, and he was very good with them. The only time Charmaine got out of bed was to shower, use the bathroom, and to give her kids a bath later that night. That day, it wasn't extremely cold out, so Rico bundled them up and took them to the neighborhood park. After dinner and their bath, the kids were out like a light before nine p.m. Rico laid on his stomach with his head resting on Charmaine's thighs.

"I can't believe you've been pregnant this whole time and didn't tell me. I was going to ask you when your period came on. I was hoping it wouldn't be here on Valentine's Day. Do you want a boy or a girl?" He looked up at her.

"I already have one of each, so it really doesn't matter. Boys can be very hype and a handful, but little girls can be spoiled and bratty at times. I can't even say which gender is best." She laughed. "But if I absolutely had to pick, I'd say I want another boy."

"I think I would like a boy too. Get a little junior popping out here in these streets." Rico kissed her thigh.

He placed small pecks all the way up until he got in between her legs. He slid her shorts and panties off, and Charmaine gasped as his mouth covered her vagina. Rico ate pussy like a professional porn star, and she loved it. He gave her the perfect balance of licking and sucking. Sometimes, he sucked her so soft and slow, it felt as if he was doing it in slow motion. Charmaine left puddles so large in the bed after her sex sessions with Rico, sometimes she had to wonder what in the world he did to her body. She had never been a squirter before, but Rico had her busting off like a water gun from his mouth and his dick game.

"I love you. You know that, right," he spoke into her pussy just as it began to contract.

"I love you too," she whimpered as she came.

"Ummmmm." Rico didn't let up on her, and he moaned as she released ,causing her to tremble.

He laid on his back and let her get on top. Charmaine figured she was emotional because she was pregnant, but she felt herself fighting back tears as she looked down at him. Two men had come into her life with lies and games and left her alone with kids to raise on her own. She had no faith left in men, but Rico came along and showed her that good men absolutely still existed, and that turned her on more than his full lips, his thick dick, his bulging muscles, and his good looks. Charmaine had so many orgasms when she had sex with Rico because she was head over heels in love with him. It was a mental thing, and he had her head fucked all the way up, but she loved it. As she rode him and stared into his eyes, she felt her pussy muscles contracting yet again. "I fucking love this good ass pussy," he whispered, and she came instantly.

"Oh my God," she breathed hard as she came. Rico grabbed her waist and thrust his hips, so that he was fucking her hard and fast even though she was on top of him. Charmaine had to lean over and bite the pillow because she didn't want to wake her kids up.

"This my pussy, forever, right?" Rico grunted, and all she could do was nod.

Their lips connected, and her tongue probed his mouth as he smacked her on the ass over and over again. That caused orgasm number three to rip through her body and that time, they came together. "I don't know how many kids you want," Rico panted when she got up off of him, "but unless you want to be pregnant every six months, you gon' need some birth control for sure."

As long as he could provide and remained a good solid man, and as long as her pregnancies were easy like this, Charmaine would give Rico as many babies as he wanted.

THE NEXT DAY, CHARMAINE ROLLED HER EYES WHEN SHE SAW WHO was calling her. She had gotten out of class for the day and was headed for the grocery store.

She almost ignored it, but right before it could go to voicemail, she answered in an icy tone. "Hello?"

"Are you really going to let my son go to prison? He didn't put that hoodlum of yours back in prison when he was beat up a few weeks ago. Broken nose, eye swollen shut! But you shot my baby and had him arrested?"

Charmaine frowned up her face. "A few weeks ago, my man was in prison, so I don't know what your hoe ass son told you, but don't call me with that bullshit. And you're just as sorry as he is! I see why he's a deadbeat. You don't call my phone to check on your grandson but you call trying to defend your loser of a son. He kicked in my door with a ski mask on his face. You're damn right I shot him, though, I didn't know it was him at the time. And I'm not sorry! Fuck your son, and fuck you too!" The woman gasped just as Charmaine hung the phone up in her face.

It's like she could only go one or two days having peace. After a few days of normalcy, drama would rear its ugly head, and she was over it. Charmaine grabbed some food to cook for dinner, some snacks, and some Valentine's Day candy and balloons. She was going to make baskets for her kids. Charmaine loved Valentine's Day, and even when she was single, she'd buy herself things and buy things for the children. This year Valentine's Day would be lit. She wasn't broke, and she had a man that she loved. At home, Charmaine stopped at the mailbox. She sorted through the bills and raised an eyebrow when she saw a letter addressed to her in pretty, feminine handwriting. There was no return address. Charmaine ripped the letter open and squinted as she read over the neat cursive writing.

You don't know me, but I work at the prison. When you and Rico were on the outs, he was definitely messing around with the female COs. Namely, me. I just didn't want you to get too involved with him and not know that he ain't the good man you think, when he's really just like the rest of these sorry ass niggas. Have a good day.

Charmaine closed her eyes and just stood there for a few seconds. When she opened her eyes back, she calmly removed her things from the car and headed inside just as Rico was stepping outside. "Why didn't you text me, so I could come and get the bags?" He took them from her.

"There are only four."

"So, that's what I'm here for." He kissed her. "How was your day?"

"It was fine until Sammy's mother called me going off about having him arrested. She said he didn't have you arrested after you beat him up a few weeks ago. But I told her you were still in prison a few weeks ago." Charmaine followed Rico inside the house.

He took the bags in the kitchen, placed them on the counter, then turned to look at her. "I'm not gon' lie to you. Ever. I had a nigga beat his ass. He violated coming here. He better be glad all the nigga did was beat his ass. It could have gone a different way."

Charmaine didn't want to talk about Sammy anymore. She really didn't care that Rico had him beat up. He deserved it. "I also just got this from the mailbox." She handed Rico the envelope and watched him pull the letter out, unfold it, and read it.

As he read, she noticed a thick vein bulging out of his neck. She figured it was safe to assume that he was angry. Rico looked up at her and sucked his teeth. "Yo, this bitch—"

Charmaine held up her hand and cut him off. "I really don't care, Rico. I saw firsthand how hard Sammy went to make my life hell simply because I was with you, you had money, and I'm happy. I would never have believed a person could be that bitter and miserable, but he proved it to me. The letter even stated that you did it when you were mad at me. You thought I had another man in here. If I let that shit ruin my day, then she won." Charmaine didn't want to think about Rico with another woman, but she was tired of people fucking with her like she didn't deserve to be happy. Charmaine refused to let outside forces ruin her relationship. She deserved this shit.

"I still want to explain. I was wrong as hell for not hearing you out and letting you explain before I took your name off the list. She saw that shit and was being nosey. I basically told her to mind her business. She called me to the laundry room and grabbed my dick and started jacking it. I was shocked, but more than that I was hurt and mad. I felt like I had just lost the only person that mattered in my life. I didn't flirt with her at all. I never gave her the impression that I wanted to fuck her. Mad niggas be on her, and I never did that corny shit. But I didn't stop her. I wasn't the aggressor, but I didn't tell her to stop. She jacked me off for a few minutes and before I came, she started sucking me off. That's it. She got mad when you came to visit me, and she was popping shit talking about how we had a quick breakup. She's salty. I swear."

Charmaine clicked her tongue. "Females are really out here thirsty like that? Wow."

"Baby, I'm sorry. I take full responsibility for not stopping her."

"It's fine, Rico. I'm not going to trip off that. It is what it is."

He looked at her to make sure she really wasn't mad. "Are

you sure? Let's talk about this now. I don't want it coming back up two days from now."

"I said it's fine, Rico. I don't want to keep talking about this. Trust me."

He walked over to her and placed his arms around her. It seemed like they kept getting obstacles thrown their way, but Rico and Charmaine were determined to overcome each and every one of them.

Chapter

SEVENTEEN

Before Charmaine even opened her eyes, the aroma of food filled her nose. When she sat up in bed, Rico, Micha, and Morgan were entering the room. Rico had a tray in his hands filled with food. "Happy Valentine's Day, Mommy." The kids ran over to the bed and jumped on it, so they could hug and kiss her.

Charmaine saw that they were already dressed for school, and she looked over at the clock. "I slept through my alarm?"

"I cut it off." Rico placed the tray in her lap. "I got the kids. I'm about to walk them out to the bus. You enjoy your breakfast."

"This is awesome, babe. Thank you so much. Have a great day at school, babies." Charmaine gave each of her kids a kiss, and Rico helped them put their coats on.

If it was one thing Ms. Mary taught Rico, it was how to cook. He could throw down in the kitchen. Charmaine's eyes swept over the scrambled eggs with cheese, avocado toast, fried beef smoke sausage with onions and peppers, cheese grits, and hashbrowns. Her mouth watered, and she quickly said her grace and dug into the food. When Charmaine was done with her breakfast, she took a shower, brushed her teeth, and combed her hair. She headed downstairs to find her man, so she could give him some morning sex, and she gasped when she entered their living room.

There was a huge life-sized teddy bear sitting on the couch. On the coffee table was a vase filled with red roses and one filled with yellow roses. There must have been thirty pink, red, and white balloons floating in the air, and the floor was basically covered in rose petals. Shopping bags and gifts lined the couch, and there were also chocolate covered strawberries on the coffee table. Rico came out of the kitchen, and Charmaine looked over at him.

"How did you do all of this?"

"You know who my right hand is when I want something executed."

Charmaine smiled. "Lauren."

"And she delivers every time. Do you like it?"

"Baby, I love it. All of this is so sweet and thoughtful. I want us to stay like this forever." Charmaine was truly happier than she'd ever been in her life. No bitter baby daddies or salty ass correctional officers could mess up what they had. The bond they were building was one that couldn't be easily broken.

"You said forever?" Rico asked.

"Forever."

He got down on one knee, and Charmaine almost fainted. Rico pulled a blue ring box from the pocket of his sweatpants, and her knees buckled. "You didn't know me or a thing about me, and you started talking to me for me. I couldn't wine and dine you, and I didn't have money to give you like that, and even with all that you had going on, you held a nigga down. You didn't miss a visit or a phone call unless it was about your job or your kids. You weren't out here on that shit that other females are on. You didn't care about clubbing or stunting for social media. You were just trying to provide a decent life for your children. Thank you for rocking with me. Thank you for trusting me and being you. You're about to give me my first child, and I want to give you my last name. Will you marry me?"

By the time he was done with his speech, tears were streaming down Charmaine's face. No one had ever said such romantic words to her before. She nodded her head feverishly, and Rico slid a square rock on her finger that made her ass do a doubletake.

"I love you so much," she cried.

Once she composed herself, Charmaine opened her gifts, and then she got a text message. Standing up she looked over at Rico with a sinister gaze.

"Well, baby, you're not the only one that can pull things off. Open the door," she instructed him.

Rico headed over to the door and when he opened it, he saw a black Range Rover that matched hers with a big red bow on it.

"You got me a car, and you didn't even have one yourself. Now, we have his and hers joints." She nearly started crying again from the thought of what he had done for her.

Rico picked Charmaine up and spun her around in the air. She was the true definition of a ride or die. After he placed her back on her feet and kissed her, Rico went outside to check out his gift. Him and Charmaine then proceeded to make love in every room of their house.

Epilogue

Charmaine gave birth to a baby boy, Rico Junior, and her and Rico got married two months later. Rico's grandmother comes over often and helps with the kids, and Sammy was sentenced to twenty-two months in prison.

The end!

Sneak Peek!

*Also Currently Available From
Essence's Bestselling Author Blake Karrington*

GOD FORGIVES
THE STREETS DON'T
by

Blake Karrington

Here's A Sneak Peek!!

Prologue

atching him walk away through unblinking eyes, I was in pain like I had never suffered before. One thing was obvious, and that was the fact that even though I had taken numerous slugs, I was still alive. With that thought in mind, I knew that if I planned to stay alive, I needed to get help immediately.

Searching the parking lot for Monique, I thought it odd that after all the gunplay that had just taken place, she hadn't come to my assistance by now. Wondering what could have become of her, I began to drag my battered body towards my car, which at the moment, was the only thing I could think to do.

Oblivious to the stares of the slowly gathering crowd, I finally made it to the car and got inside after using every ounce of strength left in my steadily weakening body. Rummaging through my blood soaked pockets, I removed my keys and attempted to place them in the ignition as I recalled the parting words of my would-be assassin: *I'll be sure to take care of your bitch!*

Old thoughts of past friends and foes came to me as I lingered between coherence and oblivion. With every breath I took, another ghost from my past would glare at me in silent disgust. The faces of the many people who had shared my path through the years crowded my headspace. Their expressions clear against the backdrop of my blurry vision.

After all I'd lived through, all that I had accomplished; it seemed inconceivable that this was how it would end. Ironic, I guess, considering all of the death sentences I had handed down to unsuspecting lames for committing my exact offense. Getting caught slipping. The hunter had become the hunted.

This was the path that I had set for myself. What I did know, is that whatever my destiny called for, I would be prepared. When it was all said and done, what was life anyway? It was nothing more than a day to day struggle to survive. And no matter how much I wanted to walk away, there was no way that I could. I had been taught at an early age that "God forgives, the streets don't!"

1991

Fresh out of jail for what I realized was more or less the fourth time, I found it hard to even enjoy the so called freedom I now had. Besides my new mentality, nothing in the free world had changed as far as I could tell. With no money, and the added responsibility of a new child on the way, I realized that the time for games had passed. Shit wasn't going to get better on its own, so I planned to force the hands of fate and come up by any means.

"It's cold out this bitch!" Sam snapped, rubbing his hands together and blowing out icy clouds of smoke. "Where the hell is this nigga at?"

Staring at his reflection in the freezing darkness, I wondered the same thing. Fingering the trigger of my .357 magnum, I gritted my teeth and chose not to give an answer to a question that neither of us could possibly know.

Feeling the vibration on my hip, I immediately forgot my previous thought and reached for the pager. Hitting the light in order to clearly see the number, I wasn't surprised to see my home number reflected back at me. The 911 code that preceded the number was only supposed to be used for emergencies. But when Monya called, in her mind, it was always an emergency.

See, Monya was my lady. She had held the title for the last seven years. Regardless of who I shared my time and body with, I had never loved another. At times like this, she had the ability to try my patience, but I guess that after seven consecutive years, it was nothing new.

Placing the pager back on my side, I surveyed the scene around me. With green fatigues on to match our beef and broccoli timbs, we fit in perfectly with the bushes we were entrenched in at the moment. The cold ground had the effect of making my freezing body ache. This also had the ability of making me angrier each minute I had to continue waiting for my unsuspecting victim.

Feeling the vibration again, I sucked my teeth in irritation. Already aware of who it was without even having to look, I reached down and turned it off. I was already aware that across the city, my baby was going to pitch a fit. But hey, if I didn't handle my business, we would never be able to experience any pleasure.

"Uhh!" Monya angrily exclaimed, tossing her arms up in a fed up manner. "I can't believe that motherfucker has the nerve to ignore my pages," she loudly snapped.

Pacing the floor, she couldn't help but envision numerous scenarios that would explain his not returning her calls. The one that came to mind was that Chez more than likely, was laid up somewhere with a trifling female.

At the thought alone, Monya began dialing his pager number again. Finding his pager cut off, only served to increase her rage. Tired of his shit, she threw the phone against the wall with all her might. Folding her arms across her bosom, Monya made a silent promise to herself that as soon as she had the baby things were going to change in their relationship.

Glancing in the mirror, Monya saw her reflection staring back. Even with an angry scowl plastered over her features, she was a true beauty. She was a little heavier than she liked, due to the pregnancy, but she was beautiful, to say the least. Staring harder, Monya noted the long, lustrous, dark silky curls that framed her almond complexioned face. Her dark, smoldering eyes had an alluring presence that gave off an exotic quality. It was the beauty mole that sat right below her thick, succulent bottom lip, right between the point of her lip and chin, which certified her as a truly gorgeous creature.

As if seeing herself for the first time, Monya chewed on her bottom lip in silent contemplation. No longer angry, the thought surfaced that if she wanted, any nigga in the city would gladly fall at her feet. They never came outright with proposi- tions, but their leering stares spoke their thoughts more clearly than any words ever could. Nevertheless, she wanted no one but Chez, and everyone knew it. Plus, his ass was known to act a fool, and niggas in the city were well aware that to mess with her was a guaranteed invitation for bloodshed.

Smirking, she poutingly stated, "You make me sick, nigga."

Running her manicured nails through her tresses, Monya plopped down on the foot of their bed. There was no getting around the fact that she was hopelessly in love. The worst part was, she had no control over her heart.

I WAS BEGINNING TO WONDER IF I'D BEEN SENT ON A DUMMY mission as I looked at my watch. The nigga was over an hour late and I was freezing. After waiting in the cold all this time, I'd made up my mind that the bitch, Qwena, was wearing an ass whipping if her information turned out to be bogus.

139

Before I'd even finished having the thought, Sam signaled to let me know our vick had arrived. Turning in the direction of the loud music, I spotted the Cherokee and driver we'd awaited. The word on the wire was that he had cake. If that was the case, he would soon find out what happens when someone else wants your dough more than you. I was about to be on some pay me or pay the devil a visit shit real soon.

The Geto Boy's track, "My Mind Playing Tricks on Me," played at a deafening tone as he pulled into his driveway. Rico took his time exiting the vehicle. Slamming the door, he activated his key alarm before walking up the sidewalk with a shiny chrome 9 millimeter swinging by his side.

Watching from the shadows, it was amusing to me that his punk ass was trying to pimp as if he was tough. Signaling to Sam, I set the robbery in motion no sooner than Rico began to place his key in the door.

Turning his key, Rico heard footsteps approaching from behind. Alarmed, he attempted to turn in the direction of their approach. Before he could do so, a vicious blow to the back of his head from a heavy object, sent him reeling through the open door. Howling in pain, it took him a moment to register what had taken place.

Opening his eyes, Rico found himself staring down the barrel of a gun. I almost laughed out loud as Rico's eyes bulged when he saw me holding the gun. When he noticed Sam enter the house behind me, the look of terror on his face intensified. He seemed ready to vomit, shit himself, or both.

"I caught your ass slipping, didn't I, nigga?" I spat coldly.

Before Rico could respond, I said, "You know what it is. Now what's it gonna be, a robbery or a homicide?"

Thumbing back the hammer on the magnum, I patiently awaited Rico's answer.

We watched as his internal struggle played out in his features.

I bet that nigga is wondering how we found where he lays his head, I thought with a smirk. I could tell that his punk ass was afraid to die, and he already knew that I could pump him full of lead and go have a sandwich.

I WASN'T SURPRISED WHEN HE STAMMERED "YOU CAN HAVE IT ALL, man."

Disgusted with Rico's weakness, I smacked him in the head with the pistol for the hell of it. In a flat, even tone, I said, "Lay all that shit out then, nigga. And just in case you try to play me, know that I'll gladly leave your ass leaking up in this bitch!"

"You don't have to hurt me, Chez. I'll get it, man."

Staring at him through beady eyes, I hissed, "Get my shit then, bitch!"

Holding his man down, Sam watched Rico like a hawk. One false move, and he would gladly let both barrels go on the sawed off. Known for having an itchy trigger finger, it wouldn't take much for that particular thought to become a reality. Sucking his teeth, he grinned at the sight before him.

I matched his grin, knowing that we were having the same thought. The nigga was just strolling cockily as if he had killer in his blood. Now, only minutes later, here he was crawling through the house on hands and knees with tears in his eyes.

Shaking his head, Sam mumbled, "The shit never fails."

TIRED OF DIALING CHEZ'S NUMBER, MONYA CURLED UP ON THE bed and hugged a pillow protectively. She felt so lost and alone. After all the years she and Chez had been together, it would seem that she would be accustomed to his disappearances, but that wasn't the case. When he wasn't in jail, which was seldom, he was still basically missing in action. Yet, she never strayed; always remaining faithful and trustworthy.

Monya could still recall the first time they met. He had been so handsome, in a rugged type of pretty boy way. His short, wavy hair, cinnamon complexion and hazel eyes were an immediate turn on for her. At 5 foot 9 he wasn't too tall, but his strength of character made him a prominent presence in her eyes.

Once they had become an item, Monya was in awe of the many stories he shared with her. From seeing his parents get murdered before his eyes, to growing up in countless foster homes, he'd experienced more than his share of suffering. These stories only served to solidify their relationship.

In Monya, Chez was able to find someone he could finally love and trust. Monya had found her soul mate in him, as well as someone who truly needed her.

Even now, when the road was somewhat rocky, she still felt that they shared their beginning bonds. Hopefully, when their child arrived, things would get better. Feeling the tears beginning to cloud her eyes, Monya sadly realized that they couldn't continue to live this way.

"NIGGA, WHAT THE HELL IS THIS?" I ANGRILY QUESTIONED. "Eight grand and three punk ass ounces. You have got to be kidding." Slapping Rico in the face with the butt of my pistol, I snapped, "Where's the rest of it?"

Grabbing his badly bloodied face, Rico howled in pain. "I gave you everything I had, man. I swear to you, I wouldn't hold nothing back, Chez."

Pacing around the room, I had to take a moment to swallow his words. More than likely, he hadn't withheld anything, but in no way did that change the thoughts that now ran through my mind.

Catching Sam's eye, I silently conveyed my thoughts to my partner. Without having to say a word, Sam received the message that Rico was taking his last breaths at that very moment.

Breaking our stare, I swiveled to face Rico. Raising the Magnum, I began to speak in a slow, calculated tone. "Being that you only had eight grand and three ounces, I feel like you wasted my time. You already know I can't allow that, right?"

Throwing his hand's up in a futile attempt at blocking the shells that were now inevitable, Rico sobbed loudly. "Don't do this, man! Please don't do..."

Cutting his pleas short, I fired two well-placed slugs into Rico's throat. The force of the closely fired slugs severed the left side of his neck. With eyes that bulged out in shock, Rico wheezed loudly in an attempt to breathe. Squirming erratically in a quickly increasing pool of blood, he spewed a miniature blood fountain with each forced breath.

Having seen enough, I turned to walk away. Nodding my head in Rico's direction, I nonchalantly mumbled, "Finish him, bro."

Without hesitation, Sam walked over to Rico who was only seconds away from death, and let the sawed off roar. Without even giving him a second glance, Sam calmly strolled out the door. In his mind, it was all part of a day's work. Murder was never personal with him, bodying a nigga was strictly business.

ROLLING THROUGH THE STRIP, WE PUFFED ON A SPLIFF OF GOOD green while acknowledging our people who held the block down by whatever means necessary. Raised within the same streets, I knew the rules and respected all those who played the game in the same manner as myself. Weak dudes were excluded; as an unwritten rule, if I was hungry they weren't allowed to eat. But in my hood, weak dudes weren't the norm. We prided ourselves on raising soldiers in the 3rd Ward, and that's just the way it was.

Whipping into the alley, my thoughts came to a halt. Before my eyes, the street opened into what resembled a block party. Wall to wall cars inched their way through the packed street. Ballers and the usual baller chasers were in attendance. A light sprinkling of junkies could be seen within the crowd, politicking in hopes of a quick hit or fix. Grinning inwardly, I exhaled a cloud of weed smoke as I pulled to the curb.

Handing the spliff to Sam, I said, "You ready, player?"

"You know I am," he exited the car to the sound of a female calling out to him.

Deciding that he would be held up for a while, I figured I'd go on without him and just catch up later. Making my way through the congested crowd, I was halted numerous times before reaching the spot. Between giving pounds to my homies and receiving numerous hugs from countless thick hoodrats, I thought I'd never make it through the door.

Once inside, I wasn't surprised to find that the crowd was standing room only. Nor was I surprised to see the crowd parting so that I could get through. Reaching the bar, I had to grin at the fact that in my city, I was the shit.

TURNING AROUND WITH TWO DRINKS IN HER HANDS, AND HER usual evil look in place, Kim laid eyes upon me. Her hard features immediately softened. Setting the drinks on the bar, Kim smiled. "Hey there, Chez. What you drinking tonight, baby?"

"What's up, boo? Give me a double gin and fix yourself something on me, alright?"

Winking her eye in a seductive fashion, she responded, "Your double gin's coming up. While I'm at it, I think I will take you up on that free drink."

Nodding my head in agreement, I sternly watched her walk away. Swiveling on the stool, I scanned the crowd to see if I could spot any of my crew in the place. Seeing no one, I heard Kim set my drink down on the bar behind me.

Turning back to face her, I took a sip from the drink, then asked, "Are any of my people in here, ma?"

"Umm Hmm. I haven't seen Dresser, but Boo-Boo and Satin are back there in the crap room."

Turning up my drink as I stepped off the stool, I said, "Thanks, ma." Flinging a 20 on the bar, I added, "Keep the change, and don't spend it all in one place either."

Smirking, I walked away, but not before her reply caught me.

"Pssst, big fucking spender!" Laughing, Kim loudly advised, "Don't get in no shit tonight either, nigga!"

Reaching the back room, Satin's voice was the first and loudest I heard. Flanked by two dime pieces, he shook his hand feverishly, making the two dice he held tightly in his grasp clack audibly. Realizing that regardless of how loud they clacked, he had them locked. I awaited the set shot that all the silent onlookers were apparently dumb to.

"You niggas ready for this? Huh? Let me know something," he said, goading his opponents. Releasing the dice, he chuckled, "Seven, bitch!" Reaching around the board, Satin arrogantly stated, "That's right, pay me."

Shaking my head, it was funny to me how my dude had a knack for hustling hustlers and mackin' chicks. Even now, two women possessively held on to him as if he only belonged to them singularly. Without a doubt, Satin had to be the smoothest nigga I'd ever met, hands down. Locking eyes with Boo-Boo in the crowd, I started moving in his direction.

Boo-Boo and Satin were cousins. Like Satin, Boo-Boo also had game. The only difference between the two was Boo-Boo went hard. When shit got crazy, he was the one I wanted in my corner. While Satin was the player in their family, Boo-Boo was the gangster. It was a well-known fact throughout the city that when I went, he went; the other way around held just as true.

"What up, nigga? Where you been?" he questioned, never taking his eyes off Satin or the dudes crowded around him.

Following his eyes, I replied, "There was a little cash sitting in a motherfucker's safe that was in need of another home, so I had to make a run to pick it up."

Smirking, he cut his eyes in my direction. "Oh yeah? Why you ain't give me a holler, huh? It's like that now?"

"Nah, it ain't like that at all, Bro. Shit was sweet, and Sam was already with me, so there was no need to run around searching for you."

Narrowing his eyes, he spoke through clenched teeth. "Damn! You took that pretty nigga with you? You're lucky he didn't fuck around and get you killed."

Shrugging my shoulders carelessly, I ignored his comment, deciding to just let it go at that. Turning to scan the crowd and women in it, I thought to myself that there was definitely no love lost between the two of them. It was no mystery that Boo-Boo and Sam didn't get along.

As far as Boo-Boo's pretty boy comment, it only held true on the outside, because Sam had killer stamped all over his heart and mind. All who knew Sam, realized that the green eyed, light skinned nigga was far from soft. His hands and guns were official as they came.

"Yo, Boo-Boo, you seen any of my bitches up in here, man?"

"Yeah. The thick red bitch you bagged at Tracy's was up at

the bar earlier. I know you're not tripping, but the nigga Herb was all up in her face on some fake mackin' shit."

"That nigga won't let a bitch live. If he don't do shit else, he will fuck something," I laughed, thinking that as long as it wasn't Monya that he was trying to get at, I couldn't care less.

As far as Missy was concerned, Herb hadn't done anything wrong. She was a bad bitch and he was supposed to try to get at her. Satin's voice interrupted my train of thought.

Flashing a large knot of bills, Satin boisterously stated, "I'm breaking these lames, bro. They don't have a clue, dog."

Extending my hand for our customary pound, I grinned. The grin wasn't so much for the words he had just spoken; it was due to the devious thoughts running through my mind. Even though I'd never play my man by trying to snag one of his women, I couldn't help the wicked thoughts I was having. If he offered, I'd gladly punish either one of the delicious looking females on his side.

Snapping out of my thoughts, I said, "We need to talk, bro."

"Not a problem, my nigga." Peeling bills from the knot he'd been flashing, Satin spoke in each of the female's ears before handing them the money and sending them on their way.

Turning back to face me, he said, "Okay what's on your mind, Chez?"

Taking a moment to formulate my words, I blurted out, "It's time to ante up and get this dough, player. Money is flowing through here like never before, and it's our time to come up in a major way, man."

"I'm already straight, bro. Right now, I can't see how shit could possibly get any better than this," he replied boisterously.

How did I know his petty ass would be on some 'I' shit? It always seemed to be strictly about Satin, and I was sick of it. Holding my rising temper in check, I decided to try a more diplomatic approach.

"Yeah, you're that nigga." I replied in a mocking tone. "Only thing is, why should you keep getting all these other niggas rich, copping weight for outrageous prices, when we can go up top and cop our own shit? Roll with me, nigga. I'm telling you, we can really blow."

Sighing, Satin looked everywhere but at me when he spoke. "You got a damn good idea, Chez, but I was always taught that if it ain't broke, don't fix it." Fidgeting, he threw it out there, "Let me stack some more dough, and in a couple months, we'll see, alright?"

"Yeah, Alright then," I answered, wanting to slap the shit out of his selfish ass.

I was willing to wait a couple months, but with or without him, it was going down. I was hungry, and if I had to die in order to reach my goals this time around, that was a price I was willing to pay.

Chapter Two

Covered in sweat, I released Missy's hips and watched as she sprawled flat out on her stomach. Even with her hair disheveled, she was a sight for sore eyes. Reaching for my boxers, I admired the back shot that was so inviting. Inviting or not, it was time to hit the road. The sun was my worst enemy, and the last thing I needed was for it to come up before I made it home.

Wiping a long wisp of hair out of her eyes, Missy looked over her shoulder and spoke in a sexy, teasing manner. "Where you going, Chez? We're not hardly finished yet, boo."

Grinning slyly, she turned on her side so that all her goodies were showcased properly.

Hesitating momentarily, my eyes were involuntarily glued to the delicious sight she presented, laying there looking like a video model. My bigger head won the battle, strengthening my resolve to get home to the video model that really counted. Shrugging my shoulders in a manner that basically said 'I'm sorry', I responded with five words that always had the ability to turn a female's smiles into frowns. "I gotta go home, ma."

Sucking her teeth loudly, Missy rolled her eyes, turned her back and buried her face in the pillow.

Making my way to the bathroom for a well needed shower, I thought, *oh well, if she didn't know by now, she should have.* No woman came before, Monya. Whether she chose to respect it or not, was her option. But like all the rest, I had no doubt that she would play the game by my rules.

ARRIVING AT HOME, I GLANCED UPWARD. I'D BEAT THE SUN THIS time, but the burnt orange texture of its appearance was slowly creeping through the darkness of night as I exited the car. Strolling towards the house, I was sure that Monya would be wide awake and in wait of my entrance. Placing my key in the door, I prepared myself for the argument that I knew was coming.

Opening the door, I sighed slightly at the sight of Monya's silhouette sitting motionless on the couch, in the dark. "Hey baby. What you doing sitting in the dark?"

"Hey baby, my ass!" she snapped, jumping up from the couch. "Where the fuck have you been, Chez? Why the hell is your pager turned off?" she blurted out angrily, pointing her finger accusingly.

Cutting my eyes evilly at the finger that was only inches from my face, I concluded that her argument would fade if I ignored her. Tossing my keys on the counter, I walked past her as if she wasn't even standing there.

"Nigga, don't ignore me!" she ranted, stalking my every step.

Reaching the bedroom, I perched on the edge of the bed and began to remove my boots. Tuning out her angry taunts, I tossed them in the closet. With her damn near standing between my legs, removing my socks and fatigues was awkward, but not impossible.

"I'm sick of your shit, Chez! Either you get it together or I swear that when I have this baby, I'm leaving your ass," she threatened with a quivering voice and tear filled eyes.

Glancing up into her face with an incredulous look, I dropped the shirt I'd just pulled over my head. No longer able to ignore her, Monya had garnered my complete attention with her matter of fact statement.

"Huh?" I asked dumbfounded. With a stone face, I mumbled, "What did you just say, Monya?"

Subtly taking a step backwards, Monya hesitantly stated, "You heard me. I said you have to—"

Allowing my eyes to appraise my woman, I refused to even entertain the thought of her going anywhere. Leave me. Psst, never! Not in a million years would I allow that. In a zone, I took notice of the way her thick nipples pushed at the fabric of her short-shirt. Even pregnant, Monya was beautiful. Short and thick, Monya was blessed with the exotic features of a China doll. Dark, sexy eyes, cold black, long silky hair and thick, juicy thighs that connected to an award winning ass were just a few of the physical features that held my attention through the years. Even now, as I watched her mouth moving, I realized that I had to have her. Reaching outwards, I grabbed two hands full of ass and pulled her to me.

Gently biting her nipple through the thin shirt, I ignored her weak struggles. Palming her ass, I squeezed the cheeks tightly, while sucking as much of her breast into my mouth as possible. Feeling her fingers begin to roam through my hair, along with her quickened breaths, I knew we were on the same page.

Releasing my hold, I held her gaze as I removed my boxers then her shirt. With nothing on but panties, I slowly placed my thumbs in the band on both sides and began to lower them. Locking her dreamy eyes on the dick, she slowly raised one leg then the other, before stepping completely out of them.

Wrapping her hair in my hands, I pulled her body down flat on my own as our lips locked in a silent, hungry battle. Adjusting her frame further down on my torso, I felt her lips engulf the head of my dick. Unable to contain my lust, I raised my hips off the bed and buried my swollen head inside her warm tight, satiny soft insides.

"Umm" Monya groaned at the feel of the sweet invasion. Breaking the kiss, but holding eye contact, she slowly began to rotate her hips in an attempt to take as much of me inside her as possible.

Gripping Monya's ass to control the depths of my thrust, I stared into the bottomless pools of her dark eyes. I could honestly say that she was the only woman I ever loved, and at times like this, I couldn't quite understand why I gave myself to any other besides her.

Arching her back, Monya got all the way into the ride she was experiencing. "Mmm, Chez. You... feel...so...good...baby!" she whimpered, bucking up and down on the dick with her head thrown back in ecstasy.

Meeting her stroke for stroke, I held her swollen, jiggling breast with the nipples trapped tightly between my index and middle fingers. Feeling her pace quicken, it was evident due to her moans and the loud slapping sounds her ass was making every time it connected with my thighs, her climax was rapidly approaching.

"Chez, Chez. Oh, shit! Damn, Baby!" Monya whimpered, leaning back to grasp my thighs with her eyes clamped tightly.

Trembling, on the brink of cumming myself, I sadly experienced a twinge of jealousy at the thought of my boo riding another nigga like this. Umph umm! I wasn't hardly gonna allow that to happen. Right then, I decided that from this moment on, it was strictly gonna be about Monya and our child. There would be no more bullshitting in the streets with loose, gold digging females. Feeling Monya's juices pouring over me with her pulsating climax, I closed my eyes to the realization that although I meant what I was saying, a new day was arriving with the coming sun. The only question that ran through my mind as I shot my second load of the night into my baby was *how would I feel when the new day arrived?*

Chapter Three

Awakening, I rolled over and glared through slits at the clock that sat on the dresser. Needing to get out of bed, I couldn't seem to make my body work along with my mind. Although the clock read 1:40 PM, after murdering a nigga, sexing two women back to back, and not getting to sleep until the break of day, I was truly exhausted.

Exhaling, it was apparent that I had too many tasks that needed to be attended to, so I removed the covers and sleepily sat up in bed. Reaching for my cigarettes and vibrating pager in the same motion, I squinted my eyes to see who was blowing me up. Frowning at the number that continuously popped up on the screen, I tossed the pager back on the night stand with no intention of returning the call.

Sparking the Newport, I had to shake my head at the thought of Qwena's worrisome ass sweating a nigga all early and shit. After giving up the whereabouts of Rico's crib, she was ready to get broke off. Oh, well. As far as I was concerned, the nigga never came home. Releasing a cloud of smoke, I grinned at the thought of her never receiving a dime of my blood money. Fuck her! She wasn't new to the game, so her trifling ass shouldn't have a problem with taking the loss.

Puffing on my first Backwood of the day, I whipped through the city as if the streets belonged to me. Reaching over to raise the volume on the stereo, I leaned further back in the seat as the euphoric feeling of the weed seemed to suddenly take effect. Other than the fact that I had no license, I was actually feeling pretty good. Between the money that was weighing down my pockets, and the plans I had to flip it into a dynasty, I couldn't see how anything could spoil my mood.

On that note, I figured that maybe it would be sensible to grab myself a driver so that I could ride trouble free. Dresser was the first face that popped into my mind; the only thing he loved more than looking fly, was driving. Immediately changing my route, my new destination was Dresser's crib.

Arriving at his house, I hit the horn. Seeing the door open, I wasn't surprised when Monica's nosey ass stepped outside in a pair of shorts that emphasized her every curve. Gawking openly at the sight before me, I couldn't help admiring how finely she was put together. Monica was a true cutie and she damn well knew it.

Sashaying to the car, she seductively ran her tongue over glossed lips, before saying, "What's going on, Chez?"

Smiling at her obvious flirting, I replied, "You know me, shawty." And she did, because before my man came along, I had hit it a few times myself. "Where's my man, ma?"

Frowning at the mention of Dresser, Monica replied, "You already know he's in there doing his usual. Nothing."

Laughing at her reply, I couldn't help thinking that the disrespectful bitch was too much for my man. In my opinion, she was in need of some raw discipline, but control was something he was definitely lacking when it came to women.

Prancing back towards the house, she smiled before asking, "You coming in or do you plan to keep staring at my ass?"

Caught, I got out the car and followed her inside. Trying to ignore her body, I found the task entirely too hard to even bother. Our close proximity made it impossible not to scrutinize the jiggle that was taking place beneath her thin, cotton shorts. Shaking my head, I had to snap out of the trance her ass had placed upon me.

Entering the den, I spotted Dresser watching television. Giving him a pound, I said, "What you planning to do today, my man?"

"I ain't doing shit. Why? What's up?" he questioned with little enthusiasm.

Taking a second to scan his attire, it seemed odd to me that the nigga wore every piece of jewelry he owned. He was dressed fly enough for a night out at an exclusive club and didn't have any plans besides watching television.

Snapping out of my thoughts, I said, "You trying to roll with me?"

The questioning look I saw him toss in Monica's direction had me puzzled. It seemed as if he actually needed her to make the decision for him. Staring from one to the other, I disgustedly waited to see just how the situation would play out.

Popping her lips, Monica rolled her eyes, "Hell yeah, he's trying to roll with you. Take him on a stick-up or something before you bring him back too. We need some money up in this bitch!" She mumbled, "He needs to do something instead of sitting up in my face all day," as she strutted out the room.

Wishing that he would slap the shit out of her, I watched his shoulders slump in defeat as he turned to me and stated, "I'm rolling with you, dog."

Smiling sarcastically, I said, "It pretty much seems that way. Now don't it?"

Riding through the hood, I spotted Sam in an alleyway holding one of his pits. Pointing towards him, I said, "Pull over there, Dresser."

Glancing at our approach, the gathered crowd went back to doing what they were involved in when they saw that it was only us. Coming to a stop near the alley, I rolled the window down and called out to Sam, "Yo, come take a ride with me, Bro."

Handing the chain and dog to one of the homies, Sam jumped in. Inhaling the aroma, he reached for the Backwood.

"What's up with you, nigga?" he asked, before leaning back and drawing on the weed.

"You're what's up, my nigga," was my reply as I tossed an ounce and two grand in the back seat. "Yo, Kid, you already know we came up on some short shit last night, so I'm gonna have to make your cut up later. I got to make some major moves with the rest of the loot, cuz. You already know I got you when shit gets straight, alright?"

"Man, you already know I ain't trippin'." Counting the money, he said, "Here, Bro, flip this ounce with the rest of what you got."

Reaching over the seat, I gave him a pound. "That's what's up, dog. You can believe me when I tell you, we're gonna come up big off this little shit. I'm telling you both, this is it."

"Yeah, yeah. I believe you, nigga. Now take me back around the way. I got shit to do," Sam laughed.

Grinning at what Sam said, I was just imagining what my niggas would be saying when my plans were no longer plans, but our everyday reality. When it was all said and done, I'd make believers out of everyone.

After dropping Sam off, we decided to hit the mall. I wanted to buy something nice for Monya. She deserved it, and I figured a gift would help to smooth over any irregular thoughts she may have been harboring behind last night.

Strolling through the crowded mall, I was treated to a buffet of some of the baddest females in the city. Some I knew, and the rest were prospects that I would have liked to get to know. That is, if I hadn't made the promise to myself that I was going to refrain from messing around with other chicks.

Taking a deep breath, I made an unspoken oath to stay focused. I continued walking, ignoring the flirtatious stares that were being thrown my way, from every direction. Heading into Victoria Secret, my steps were halted at the sound of someone loudly calling my name. Turning around, I came face to face with the last person I'd expected to encounter.

"You can't return my calls no more, nigga?" Qwena loudly questioned in a stink voice. Ready to cause a scene, she began to point her index finger as if it were a gun. "Let me tell your red ass something..."

"You're just the bitch I've been looking for!" I snapped, cutting her words short as I turned the tables on her. Moving with the speed of light, I glared viciously as I grabbed her throat. Wanting to laugh at the fear that was suddenly evident in her wide eyes, I hissed, "What kind of games you trying to play with that bogus ass information you gave me? Do you take me for a motherfucking chump or something, shawty?"

Nervously blinking, she began to stutter, "Uh, what...you...talking...about...baby?" Lowering her voice, Qwena apologetically stated, "I'd never try to play you, boo. Believe me."

Mean mugging, I inwardly grinned at the picture she presented. No longer loud or arrogant, she was soaking up my act like a sponge. Catching the eyes of her assembled entourage, it was apparent that they too were buying my show of anger by the way they averted their eyes when I glared in their direction.

"Look. Don't ever pull any shit like that again. You hear me?" I menacingly stated.

"I won't," she responded agreeably. With downcast eyes, she said, "I could have sworn I gave you the right address though. Plus, I've been calling him all day and he hasn't returned my messages yet. That's why I figured you got to him, boo."

Averting my eyes at her truthful words, it was hard to keep a straight face. "Nope, he never came to where I was. I missed him this time. But for future reference, I'd suggest that the next time you feel like stepping to me with some bullshit, you miss me as well," I spat, releasing my hold on her throat.

Before she could reply, Dresser gave me the exit I'd been searching for. "Let's roll, Bro. You know we got shit to take care of."

Acknowledging his statement with a nod, I said, "I'll holler at you, ma."

Turning to walk away, I felt a light tug on my jacket. Thinking, *what now?* I glanced behind me to find Qwena staring expectantly at me.

"Can I see you later, Chez?" Locking eyes with me, she ran her tongue over a pair of the loveliest full lips ever. "I promise to make it worth your while."

Weakening rapidly, I found it impossible to ignore the gesture she made with her tongue. Not to mention the fact that her promise of making it worth my while had been proven on too many occasions for tonight to be an exception. So much for my oath of monogamy. I was hitting her sexy ass before the night was over and it hadn't even been twenty-four hours since I made my vow.

"Yeah. I think we may just be able to link up, ma. I'll call you with the time later, alright?"

Grinning, she enthusiastically stated, "I'll be awaiting your call, baby."

Walking off, I noticed the smirk that was plastered upon Dresser's face.

159

Smiling myself, I inquired, "What? Why you looking like that, dog?"

Shaking his head, Dresser replied, "You never cease to amaze me man. Regardless of how badly you treat these silly bitches, they still be sweating you."

Shrugging my shoulders, I couldn't argue with the truth. Some of us have the gift, and others don't. I was just blessed with the ability to control females, without giving them the ground that I knew they would use to turn the tables on me, if given the chance. As far as I was concerned, you either ran the show or got run over. Living by that rule, I refused to falter in my game, regardless of who liked it.

After dropping Dresser off, I wasn't trying to bump into the boys in blue, so I stuck to the back streets and made sure to duck all drug zones on the way home.

Bopping my head to the sounds pouring through the system, I was interrupted by the vibration I felt on my hip. Unsnapping the miniature box from my side, I was presented with a familiar number. Before I could replace it, the vibration began again. Glancing back at the screen, I wasn't surprised to see that it was Monya again. Tossing the pager on the passenger seat, it dawned on me that this same scene had been played out in the exact manner months before. Drifting back in time, I found myself reflecting upon the events of that seemingly long ago day.

5 MONTHS PRIOR

TOSSING THE PAGER ON THE PASSENGER SEAT, I EXHALED IN AN attempt to calm the building irritation I experienced each time Monya paged me. Knowing I needed to call her back, I decided instead to wait until I got home. I was almost there already, so what difference would a few more minutes make?

Entering our neighborhood, I couldn't quite figure out what it was, but something just didn't feel right. It was as like an eerie feeling of lurking doom somewhere up ahead. Ignoring the signs, I pulled in front of our house and exited the whip in a hurry. Before I'd taken a dozen steps, it seemed as if the entire street had broken out in chaos. Men ran at me from every direction, screaming orders, with weapons drawn. Caught off guard, I could do nothing but sprawl out on the ground, place my hands behind my head, and angrily glaring at the horde of U.S. Marshals and A.T.F. agents that surrounded me.

I was immediately extradited back to Maryland, where I was arraigned on charges stemming from a case I'd caught a year earlier. From the way it looked, the feds were planning to make me sorry for ever carrying the Mac 11 nine millimeter with infrared scope and 500 rounds of ammo up the highway. Things were definitely looking dire, and without a bond, Baltimore jail had become my home. The mice and rats that ran rampant through its halls were the family I'd been given.

Down and out, with little to no hope for a change in my new reality, I was granted a gift from God. After four and a half months, my case was dropped due to a technicality. Unbelievably, I was free to pick up where I'd left off. After facing a lengthy stay in the federal penitentiary, I'd been granted a reprieve. After what I'd experienced, I made up my mind that the time had come to get what was owed to me in the game. The new me had been born, and it was on...

Snapping out of my reflection as I pulled on my street, I noticed that unlike the day in my thoughts, everyone was out and about. Before the car had even come to a complete stop, Monya opened the door and stepped outside. No longer irritated with her blowing up my pager, it suddenly dawned on me that the woman before me had been through pure hell with me through the years, while a lesser woman would have bailed on her man long ago.

Reaching for her gift in the passenger seat, I stepped from the vehicle. Seeing the slight smile that replaced the frown once embedded in her features, as she glanced from the Victoria Secret bag back to my face, I slowly cracked a smile as well.

Holding her lingering gaze, I hoped that she would never lose the faith that she held in me; it was warranted this time. With the six grand and three ounces in my possession, I was about to take our standard of living to an elevated level. As if awakening all over again, I needed no clock this time to inform me that I had much that needed my attention. It was written in stone, so I would tackle the come-up task with an intensity that was inhuman until I reached my goal.

The full novel is available on Amazon.com
God Forgives the Streets Don't by Blake Karrington

About the Author

Blake Karrington is a Essence Magazine® #1 Bestselling novelist. More than an author, he's a storyteller who places his readers in action-filled moments. It's in these creative spaces that readers are allowed to get to know his complex characters as if they're really alive.

Most of Blake's titles are centered in the South, in urban settings, that are often overlooked by the mainstream. But through Blake's eyes, readers quickly learn that places like Charlotte, NC can be as gritty as they come. It's in these streets of this oft overlooked world where Blake portrays murderers and thieves alike as believable characters. Without judgment, he weaves humanizing back stories that serve up compelling reasons for why one might choose a life of crime.

Readers of his work, speak of the roller coaster ride of emotions that ensues from feeling anger at empathetic characters who always seem to do the wrong thing at the right time, to keep the story moving forward.

In terms of setting, Blake's stories introduce his readers to spaces they may or may not be used to - streetscapes with unkept, cracked sidewalks where poverty prevails, times are depressed and people are broke and desperate. In Blake storytelling space, morality is so curved that rooting for bad guys to get away with murder can sometimes seem like the right thing for the reader to do - even when it's not.

Readers who connect with Blake find him to be relatable. Likening him to a bad-boy gone good, they see a storyteller who writes as if he's lived in the world's he generously shares, readily conveying his message that humanity is everywhere, especially in the unlikely, mean streets of cities like Charlotte.

facebook.com/bkarrington

twitter.com/blakekarrington

instagram.com/theblakekarrington

Also by Blake Karrington

Thickums

The Urban Love Series

Falling For A Hustler Like me Series

Single Ladies Series

Drunk On A Thug's Love Series

Confessions of an Urban Author Series

Trapstar Series

What Kind of Man Would I Be

Carl Weber's Kingpins: Charlotte

All or Nothing

The Best of Blake Karrington Volume 2

The Minister

Pretty Hustlaz

Counterfeit Love Series

God Forgives The Streets Don't Series

The King Of The South

Beard Gang Chronicles Series

Country Girls Series

Faith & Trust Series

Girls From Da Hood 10